DEFYING DEATH

DUTIFUL GODS
BOOK FOUR

MELISSA BELL

ACKNOWLEDGMENTS

Jordin Thiele, as always for helping to enhance my work.
(Enhancer)

&

Michele Thompson for always fixing my bads.
(Editor)

DEDICATION

~Jordin Thiele~
You take my breath away.
Love Always

*To my biggest Fangirl **Nannette Coffman**,*
thank you for all your wonderful reviews,
and your fabulous support in getting my name
out there.

PROLOGUE

Cosmo came to her son, it was that time again. Death must live among the humans for a week. It was the only way she could think of to ensure he didn't lose his compassion for the souls he collected.

Death understood this was his cross to bear, but that didn't mean he had to like it. He often wondered about his mother's reasons behind the various charades. The significance of her teachings had not been lost on him, he valued life. He didn't however, value those who abused it. They were the one's Death was never gentle with.

The worst part of this deal was that he never knew what he was walking into. He'd found himself in various situations in the past, that made him wonder if he was a sick game set up to amuse his mother.

He'd been a gladiator. After fighting for a week-long life, he had been poisoned by a guard that had money riding on his opponent. His opponent had proceeded to run him through like a succulent roast, cooked to perfection after being tenderized and beaten like a piñata. He'd collected the guard and the opponent's souls the following week after they had been put to death for match-fixing. He may or may not have influenced the way they died, but he would admit he had enjoyed the show. He would also be the first to admit, he had a vindictive nature.

In one life, he'd been a farmer who was put to the death by a greedy king, for failing to pay taxes and surrender his entire crop to the palace. Shortly after, the king was taken ill by a mysterious ailment that took his life. His kingdom was returned to the people as the king hadn't been able to sire an heir. His widowed queen went on to remarry. She lived long enough to see her son become a king of the people.

He'd also been a knight killed in battle over the borders of neighboring kingdoms, which were ruled by two cousins that always wanted what the other had. So, as a result, he gave them both syphilis, from the same woman. Who could say if it was the disease that killed them or the concoctions their physicians kept feeding them trying to heal them?

He never knew where he was going, or how he would die. He only knew that some of the people he met along the way could have been his friends in another lifetime.

CHAPTER 1

1 *340*

The first time Vanessa saw Death, she was only sixteen years old. Her mother had summoned her to the neighbors keep to help her with a difficult birth. Abigail was barely eighteen when she was betrothed to a landowner. He was significantly older than her by around twelve years, but the bargain was struck in a dark corner of a tavern near the docks. A few gold coins and a number of rounds of bootleg whiskey, a handshake, and the deal was done. The poor girl was delivered to her new husband kicking and screaming.

At least he'd been a gentleman with her and was patient enough to wait for her cycle to begin. After she'd bled, he took her to his bed and claimed her virginity. He'd been smitten with her from the day she had arrived, and even though it was an arranged marriage, she fell in love with him in a matter of months. She'd become pregnant quickly, and they were eagerly awaiting the arrival of their first child. The breech birth was overdue according to the calculations, and she'd been in labor for a day and a half when her mother sent word that she needed help in birthing the babe.

Vanessa raced to the garden and collected all the herbs her mother had asked for, then she climbed on the back of a horse and sped to her mother's aid.

She slid down from her ride before the horse had even halted and rushed to the opening door. The sounds from the master bedroom were making her stomach roll. She heard her mother yelling over the noise

Abigail was making, "Push child, you have to push."

"I can't," Abigail whimpered, exhausted from the many hours of pain.

Vanessa brought the bag of herbs to her mother's side and touched her shoulder to let her know she'd arrived. Her mother Elanora shuffled through the satchel's contents and withdrew a small portion of bark. "Get her to bite down on this, it will help with the pain."

Vanessa moved to the head of the bed and scooped the pillows aside, then lifted Abigail under the arms to slide in behind her. Her head thrashed from side to side as she rested back against Vanessa's shoulder. Vanessa placed a firm hand on her neighbor's forehead anchoring it in place as she stuffed the bark into her mouth. "Abigail, mother says to bite it. It will help with pain."

Abigail nodded her head to show she understood.

"What next mother?"

Elanora instructed her daughter to help the woman bear down. "We need to birth this babe now!"

Vanessa placed her open hands against Abigail's swollen belly drawing large circles. With the next muscle contractions, she added extra pressure to the push. Several more and the infant was finally free of the birth canal. Abigail had stopped screaming and slumped motionless against Vanessa. The amount of blood loss was too much to save her. She passed away in Vanessa's arms. The infant, also unable to survive the process, never took a first breath or a last.

Elanora cleaned the baby and wrapped it in a blanket. "Vanessa, help me to make things presentable. I have to let Gilbert know of his loss."

Vanessa repositioned the pillows, straightened Abigail's gown and pulled the cloth over her lower body to hide the mess. She lifted the baby and placed him next to his mother and touched his cheek. A tear slid free, and she vowed she would rather die than fall in love.

* * *

Death had no idea of the year, the time, or where he was. He could hear the soft melodic voice and could feel the warmth on his bottom. He was scrunched up in a space that was too small to move. He'd kicked and tried to stretch, but it only left him tired. A constant thump, thump, thump, hypnotized him to settle down and sleep. He'd been sent to Middle Earth for his usual "Live a life, walk in their shoes," in accordance with his Mother's laws. Yet again, he was sent in blind, never knowing what to expect when he reached the human realm.

He was surrounded by warm, viscous fluid, and his hand kept getting caught in a cord attached to his belly. He felt unusually cramped, the space shrinking around him. Each time the restriction grew tighter and tighter. He panicked and knew the situation wasn't a good one. He tried to move but couldn't. Everything just seemed to fade away into nothingness.

He could hear loud noises as he lost consciousness. After many hours of restriction and confusion, he heard his Mother's voice. "Take my hand son. It's time to go home."

"But I haven't lived," he said, in his mind. Unable to breathe he began to struggle.

"Don't fight it Death. This was your

lesson to learn. Not everything that lives has a life to live," Cosmo said sadly.

She took his hand and lifted him into her arms, carrying him home to his realm. She laid him on his king-size bed, covering him with a blanket, and as his body turned away from her shivering, she reached out to touch his hair. "Don't," he hissed at her. Cosmo pulled her hand back and vanished with her eyes full of unshed tears.

The events of his latest lesson left a bitterness inside him. Sometimes he really hated his existence. He never got to create life, and he himself never really got to live one. He was trapped, with nothing to look forward to. Exhaustion, coupled with the depression associated with his duties, pulled him into a deep sleep where he wished he could sleep like the dead forever.

* * *

Elanora brushed her daughters long auburn hair with the bone comb. She braided it, joining the two sides into one long plait down her back and tied it off with a leather strip.

"Don't weep child, it is the way of the

Gods. You will discover one day, they do not discriminate. They don't care if you're of rich noble blood or a pauper. Coin cannot buy your life. The only thing you can do is live true to yourself. Live every day to the fullest, and love with all your heart when you find it. I will speak to your father when he returns from the sea. I will implore him to allow you to choose your own suitor when you find him, or he you. Now sleep child, the moon is high, it is late."

Vanessa moved from the stool she'd been sitting on, kissed her Mother's cheek and climbed into her bed. Her last thoughts were of a mysterious man with no face coming to claim her, 'I'd rather die than be a slave to love.'

* * *

Vanessa spent the following months learning about the herbs her Mother grew in the garden, in the hope that one day she would be as wise as her Mother. She knew it was her calling to try to heal the ailing and to make the journey into the afterlife less painful for those who had lived a long and full life.

The years passed by and her body became that of a beautiful ripe woman. She had many suitors come calling to ask for her hand. But each time she shook her head and said, "Nay, he naught be the one."

The following Winter, her Mother took ill with consumption. Vanessa damned the knowledge her mother had passed on, for nothing she did could heal her.

People stayed away, so as not to contract whatever Elanora's ailment was. Her Father and brothers were away at sea and had been gone for sixty moons when her mother finally succumbed to death. She sat beside her lifeless body and wept for her mother's life that had been cut short.

Death came to collect Elanora, and as he leaned over to imbibe her soul, the auburn-haired woman holding her hand lifted her head. He turned his head with her movement and felt a sucker punch to his chest. She was beautiful. He was drawn to her essence as though there was something familiar about her. She licked her lips making them shine. He became distracted by his thoughts, wondering if they tasted as delicious as they looked. He snapped out of it when her lips began to move, and it registered in his mind what she was saying. "Take me instead." Death inhaled deeply with shock at her words. His hand lifted to touch the tip of a stray curl then watched in horror as it turned grey. Nobody had ever asked a thing of him with such conviction before. His protective instincts flared, and he knew he wanted to know more about the woman that fascinated him. It was as though she knew he was in the room.

CHAPTER 2

1 *349*

HE OPENED HIS EYES TO SEE AN ANGEL hovering over him, she had magnificent eyes. She possessed the fairest of skin, with a speckling of freckles on her nose. Her auburn hair tied back in a rough bun, it looked like it was trying to break free of its confines.

He made to lift his hand so he could touch her, to see if she was real or if he was dreaming. He couldn't, he didn't have the strength. As the angel moved around him, he caught a fragrance of lavender and something else he couldn't quite make out.

"Where am I?" Death asked, confused by his surroundings.

The angel replied, "You're in my house, on the outskirts of Waterford." He recognized the lilt of tongue, he was in Ireland.

Puzzled he asked, "How long have I been here?" turning his head to cough. He felt lousy, his throat was dry, his eyes unfocused, and he was fighting not to succumb to the darkness that was trying to suck him back in.

She helped him lift his head as she spoke to him softly. "Shhhh, try to take small sips," as she placed a cup to his lips. God, the liquid tasted foul, he almost gagged. She forced him to swallow several mouthfuls of the putrid stuff before offering some water. He finally gave in to the darkness enveloping him.

He woke again, this time covered in sweat but freezing cold. As his teeth chattered together, his angel had removed his clothes and was bathing him in fragrant water.

His angel looked like she hadn't slept in a long time. The candle next to the bed swayed as she moved around, rinsing the cloth, then returning to her care for him.

"Angel, how long have I been here?" Again he asked in the hope that she would answer this time before he fell under the spell of sleep again.

"Four nights now, you have been in and out of fever," she finally replied. "It is not looking good, I'm sorry."

"Do you know what's wrong with me?" he asked. "Why do I feel so weak?"

"You suffer the Black Death. I've seen it before though I did not know what it was at the time. However, the townsfolk were told of it last week, tales of a sickness that was sweeping the mainland, brought by the merchant ships."

"I'm sorry, for I have tried everything to heal your sickness, but it would appear nothing is working." A tear ran down her cheek. He was a handsome man, even in sickness. She thought it was such a shame, a young man cut down in his prime. She knew her skills were limited and all she could do now was be there for him, to make him comfortable in his last days.

She was so tired, she'd only napped sporadically on the stool next to the bed.

She'd fought this enemy before it even had a name. Her Father and brothers had come home from working on a merchant ship. They were only with her for a day or two before they died from the mysterious ailment. Her mother passed when she was just shy of twenty.

She had no one left, she was tired. There were no eligible men, at least none she would allow to touch her. She needed to choose what to do. Did she surrender, or did she leave to find her fortune?

Time was running out, she only had a matter of days left.

Two more nights passed by with Death creeping ever closer to going home. He had experienced extreme pain, and coughing fits in the last hour had produced blood on his lips.

He tried to encourage his angel to move away from him. He didn't want her to catch what he had. As he breathed his last rattled breaths, she leaned over him, looked him in the eye and whispered, "Take me with you? Please." She kissed him like her life depended on it.

As his eyes glassed over, he screamed in his head, "NO! Live! Please live for me?"

She picked up a dagger, sliced across her palm, made a cut in his palm to match, then laid down next to his lifeless body and waited for Death.

* * *

Cosmo entered the cottage and watched on as her son took his final breaths.

She could not be seen by the living. She held her breath as she observed the young woman cut their palms and lay down beside her son.

Only when the woman fell asleep, did she move to the bed to collect her son.

She took his hand, and together, they went home.

* * *

When Death woke, he was in his own bed in his own realm. He knew this was the first time he had not wanted to die, he wanted to stay with his angel. He was furious. How dare his Mother toy with him like this? She had obviously found out about his fascination for the auburn beauty he'd often dreamt of. He rubbed his sternum where his chest ached at the memory of her gentle touch.

* * *

Vanessa woke to find she was alone. The man beside her was gone. He'd passed while she was sleeping. She lifted her hand in front of her face and found a healed scar. It hadn't been a fevered dream; she'd tried to go with him. Why had Death cheated her? Why was she still here?

Frustration boiled to life inside her. She sat up and straightened her clothes. She mumbled under her breath as she began to place her belongings in a pile. If death wouldn't come for her, then she'd go and find it.

CHAPTER 3

Vanessa made the trek to the docks and stowed away on a merchant ship. However, with limited places to hide she was discovered shortly after they left the docks. The deckhand thought he would find himself in the good graces of the Captain by presenting the lass as a gift. His hand tightened on her forearm as the boat rolled over the waves.

The Captain locked her in his quarters to oversee the first portion of the journey. Vanessa's hands were tied to the center stringer in the Captain's small room. Without the ability to reach a weapon she began to pray for death, hoping her heart would simply cease to beat before they raped her and ruined her innocence. She rested her head against the timber and held her breath as the surrounding air shifted and the temperature dropped. Her senses told her she wasn't alone.

* * *

Death kissed the forehead of the seven-year-old child claimed by a broken neck. His Mother had told him many times not to climb in the woods. This would be last time he disobeyed her wishes. He collected the young boy's soul.

As he finished his duty, the hairs on his arms stood on end, and his chest began to ache. He frowned down at the body of the boy. 'No, it is definitely not him. It's his time.' Before he could consider his body's reaction a moment longer, he was sucked through the air and deposited in a room on a ship.

Dazed and confused he turned a full circle to discover his redheaded angel. Her head was down, and he could only just make out her words, "Death be mine tonight, take me from this place with haste."

Her body hugged tight to a strut that reached from floor to ceiling in the small cabin.

Death's heart stammered as he realized it was her that had reached out and called for his presence. His body heated with the knowledge that she had summoned him, Death. Nobody had ever managed to accomplish such a task in all the years he'd been doing his duty as the Grim Reaper.

"I know you're here. Help me, please." Vanessa's words startled him. How did she know he was here? He hadn't taken on human form. He was invisible to the naked eye.

The door to the cabin opened, and a middle-aged man walked in untying his britches. "Now lass, I'll be having your payment for stowing away on my ship."

His angel began to shake her head profusely, her arms tugging at the bindings around her wrists, but they held. Death materialized taking solid form and snarled, "You touch what's mine, and you will die." In the blink of an eye, he stood between the man and his prize.

"I am Captain of the vessel, and you will hold your tongue. The wench is mine to do as I will," the Captain informed Death.

Death raised his open hand and clenched it into a fist in front of the captain's face. The man's face turned red, and his fingers clawed at his throat. "I said touch her, and you die. Now, do you understand me? I am the reaper of souls. I collect the dead and ferry them to the afterlife. Your fair is paid in full." Death twisted his wrist, and the man's neck snapped, his lifeless body crumpling to the floor.

He pulled a dagger from the man's boot and sliced through his females bindings.

"This can't be. You're dead! I watched you die," Vanessa stumbled back, her words barely above a whisper. She lifted her hand and looked at the scar. Her face grew pale, "Oh Goddess, what have I done?" Her mind raced over things she'd learned from her mother - a Druid priestess. She shivered with the realization she'd inadvertently tied herself to an immortal, a god. Of all the gods why did it have to be him? Vanessa was all about preserving the quality of life, and he was the one who took that away. She condemned her body for its reaction to his power. He'd just taken a man's life to save her purity.

Death's eyes leveled on his red-headed angel. "I can hear your thoughts, my love." His lips didn't move, but she heard his words inside her head.

Death held up his open palm to confirm he too had a scar. His body was able to heal any wounds, and she had indeed been tied to his. It was the only blemish on his perfect body, and now that he knew its significance he would wear it with pride. She had claimed him as her protector and her God. His heart would never belong to another, and he would gladly spend eternity waiting for her to come to him.

"The next time you call for me to take you from this life, it will be because you love me more than your own existence. Until then you are free to experience all you can in this realm. You will be under my protection, your heart and your virtue is mine now and in the future. If any man or woman attempts to break that bond they will die for their sins against me as your husband." His voice rang out with a deep residue that made Vanessa's legs tremble.

She locked her knees and put iron into her spine. "You sir will be waiting until the pits of hell have frozen over."

Death disappeared from sight, and she breathed a sigh of relief, only to have him reappear an inch from her. She tried to step away, but her heel hit the base of the Captain's bed, and she toppled onto her back.

Death felt his cock stiffen harder than timber as her red hair fanned out around her head. Her face looked shocked, and he liked the way she looked. He placed a hand on either side of her hips, palms flat on the bed beside her to avoid the temptation of touching her. "You will be under me willingly one day, and you will hold desire in your eyes to feel me buried deep within your snatch. Until that day nobody else will have what's mine. They will die from want of trying. Do you understand me?" On the last of his words, she felt a fire scorch her left hip and cried out at the intense sensation. She knew without looking that he'd branded her. The sensation was gone as quickly as it at started and she couldn't exactly say it had been painful although her lady parts throbbed and it felt similar to when she'd touched herself in pleasure. She blushed as a smirk creased the corner of his handsome face. Her hand began to lift from where it had landed, it tingled with the need to feel him. Seconds before it reached his cheek he briskly withdrew from his crouched position. "If you touch me now, I'll take you with me. I'm not that strong. I've been alone for an eternity. I won't be able to keep my end of the bargain, and I refuse to see hatred and regret in your eyes. You do not know me but you will." His voice deepened with lust. "You will one day beg for my intimate touch, on every curve of your flesh. Take this compensation I'm offering you and live... for both of us."

He locked the cabin door from the inside using just his mind. He tossed the Captain's limp body to the crew stating, "This is my ship now! I'm the captain of this crew. I am the reaper of souls, and the beauty inside my cabin will reach the mainland untouched and unharmed or you will all die a slow and painful death." All eyes widened as Death turned into mist and wove around the men on deck. He then rematerialized. "I know each, and every one of you and I will hunt you down if you disobey my order." The men cowered and mumbled, "Aye captain." bowing to their knees with a fist over their chests.

With that Death vanished.

CHAPTER 4

Vanessa was woken by the sound of someone knocking on the cabin door. "Milady, we have reached the mainland. The crew awaits your departure."

"Thank you," she called through the timber, hoping they wouldn't string her up the moment she left the safety of the room.

She opened the door to find the entire crew on bended knee with their eyes downcast.

"Please, tell your Lord that we gave you safe passage milady. Some of us men have families to feed," said the man in front of her.

"Thank you, kind sirs, I am pleased that

you heeded his warning. He too will be happy," she prayed.

With her feet back on firm ground, she made her way to the nearest inn. As she passed by humble dwellings, she noticed some of the doors had been painted, and the streets were almost empty of people. The street was slippery from recent rainfall and mud stuck to her shoes.

She found the village to be in dire need of repair. The mistress of the inn was slouched on a stool with her head down on her arm. "Pardon me milady, do you have a bed for this eve?" When the woman failed to stir, Vanessa moved closer. She noticed the shallow breaths and pallor of the woman's skin. Instantly she recognized it for what she knew it to be. The Black Death was about to claim another victim. The least she could do was make the lady of the house comfortable in her final hours. She barred the front door and checked for a room. Vanessa stoked the keep's fire and searched the kitchen's supplies. She found a large pot and filled it with water from the barrel, then hung it over the fire to boil.

She dragged a straw mattress from a room and laid it out on the floor in front of the fire. She collected up all the quilts she could find. Slowly she lifted the woman's weight off the stool, kicked it out of the way with her foot and dragged her unconscious patient to the bedding. She removed all of her clothing and sat it near the fire. She would boil the clothes later. She scampered to the supplies and found a jug of vinegar which she poured into the boiling water. She also gathered a pitcher of bootleg rum.

She tore strips of cloth to bathe the woman first in the vinegar water and then she rubbed her down with the rum. After rolling her up in all the quilts bar one, Vanessa returned to the kitchen to begin supper.

She prepared soup from the crate of vegetables on the table, cooking it over the fire. She restocked the fire to keep the warmth in the room as much as possible, then retrieved another straw mattress from one of the rooms. She curled up and fell asleep. She woke to the sound of the moans.

She crawled across the short distance to find the woman awake.

"Who are you?" she asked in a hoarse voice.

"Just a healer who has traveled a long distance from home and who is in need of a place to lay for the eve," Vanessa said shyly she introduced herself, "Vanessa is the name my mother gave me, and McDuffie is the name my father honored me with."

The older woman's eyes teared up, and her hand reached out from under her coverings, "Magda, my friends call me Magda, although I do not have many of them left. They have perished from the sickness that has beaten down the doors of the proud people of the village. 'Twas only seven moons since I lost me beloved Douglas. I don't know how I will ever manage without him, but he made me promise I would not follow him into the shadows. If not for you, I surely would have broken my word."

"Tis nothing my lady. I merely made you comfortable," she bowed her head.

Magda squeezed her hand, "Tis naught nothing, you are welcome to stay while ever you need a roof over your head and a full belly. I am no lady, and it is I who should bow before you." She smiled then added, "Don't ever be ashamed of your gifts, whether they be from your mother or your gods."

Vanessa raised her head meeting Magda's eyes, gave a brief nod of her head, and with a slight curl of her lips she smiled. She liked this woman's spirit.

Over the following week, Vanessa continued to nurse Magda back to good health. When Magda ventured out of the inn for the first time in nearly a month, her fellow villagers were amazed. They'd all thought she was done for. "The gods sent me an angel to heal this tired and weary soul. I now have a new lease on life, and a young woman I would be proud to call my daughter. She has no kinfolk left in this world, so I have claimed her as my own."

She explained to everyone how the girl was a healer. The village called on Vanessa to help the ones that were unwell with the sickness. Magda and Vanessa were held in high regard after the townsfolk never lost another soul to the Black Death.

Vanessa thrived in her new surroundings, but at night when she slept, she would see the eyes of Death watching over her. Each morning when she woke she would resolve to tell Magda that it was time for her to move on to another place, but then the instant Magda's eyes fixed on her, she didn't have the heart to open her mouth for the parting words to come out.

Three years, two months and nine days after Vanessa showed up on Magda's doorstep, she found her surrogate mother peacefully passed in her sleep overnight. She'd inherited the inn after Magda's passing, but her feet were too itchy to stay. She sold it to a neighbor for a handful of gold. She packed up her belongings to move on, though it took her many hours to leave, as all the villagers begged her to stay while loading her up with gifts for her long journey.

* * *

Vanessa stayed on the move, frequently shuffling from one village to the next, never staying in one place longer than a handful of months. It seemed that every time she began to become comfortable in her surroundings, Death would find her one way or another. She avoided making friends in the fear that he would take them away from her. She preferred to live a solitary life as much as possible. The instant she felt the shift of his presence within her vicinity, she would pack her things and make a hasty voyage to another location. Before she knew it, weeks had turned into months, months into years and years into centuries.

CHAPTER 5

Death learned patience if nothing else. Every time his beloved Vanessa was fearful, he was pulled to her location. He didn't understand it but was grateful that even if she was unaware of the power she held over him, it allowed him to continue his protection of her. Whether she wanted it or not.

Her ability to resist him was getting stronger and more resilient with every passing year. She was a stubborn born female, he wished he knew how to subdue her. Sadly, he knew if he forced her compliance, it would break her and she would spend the rest of eternity hating him.

He often envisioned her in his dreams. However, that simply made him want to chain her to his bed even more. On waking he'd always find his body hard and throbbing with lust for his wife. He'd become infatuated with her, tracking her from one town to the next.

The moment she sensed him, she would run from him again. The more he reached out to her the harder and faster she ran. He snarled at her obvious attempts to believe she could, in fact, outrun Death.

As decades turned into centuries he waited, then waited some more for her to give herself freely to him, but she never did, always choosing to run instead.

Well, at least she hadn't infuriated him by denying his right to kill those who would have taken her virginity from him. There had been six of them in total over the years.

The first to die had been three nameless bandits that had attempted to pin her youthful body to the ground. She'd known they were following her along the path and her distress had summoned him to her side. He waited and watched as they surrounded her and corralled her deeper into the woods of the unfamiliar landscape. When the first one tried to lay his hand on her, he toppled over clutching his chest. The other two had been able to gain an advantage, one had a fistful of her auburn hair, and the other was lifting her dress. That man dropped her skirt as though it were on fire to claw at his throat as he choked to death. The third one had released her hair and was running in the opposite direction when his brain began to bleed inside his skull. He lunged for the ground holding his head before he fell sideways, dead.

Vanessa had collected her things, righted her attire, slipped her shoe back on and resumed her journey. She was shaken but unharmed. That had been in the human year 1354.

The next time had been a king in the making who thought he could take advantage of his queen's chambermaid, while his wife and the future queen was pregnant. He'd died mysteriously when Death had squeezed his testicles so hard his face turned purple, and he suffocated into the next afterlife.

He'd been kept rather busy over the centuries through warring kings, and their never-ending desire to conquer their own beasts. The ego of man was a fragile and turbulent bitch, it was something his brother Wahr reveled in, as it fed power to his realm like none other. The body count always maintaining the Treasury of Souls, hence overloading Death's schedule with the battle-worn dead.

* * *

Vanessa surrounded herself with the sick warriors of warring kingdoms as they returned from battle, injured. She tried to save as many of them as possible, knowing she would never succeed in keeping Death from her door. She ignored his presence whenever he was around, focusing more on the dying.

Although she couldn't really fathom why she hardly aged, she was smart enough to know it for what it was or rather, who had caused it. She'd never been sick, not even so much as a sniffle, although she would have loved to kick Death in a, particularly sensitive area for the many centuries of monthly bleeds.

She found her reflection ripening by a year for every century that passed. She'd met some interesting people, and her wealth had exponentially grown along with her knowledge. She'd seen kings rise and fall, churches rule the rulers, and brothers betray brothers on English soil. She'd grown weary of her travels and had struck out for a new life in the Americas, only to find more feuds and wars in the new land. Not to mention they'd charged her with witchcraft on more than one occasion. All for being a midwife and traveling the roads after dark. Someone needed to explain to the church fearing folk that babies are born at Luna's command. The entire idea was preposterous. If she were a witch, she wouldn't have been out that time of night to help with birthing a babe. She would have been out at midnight instead, the witching hour, at which time she would have been gathering herbs to make the tonics and tinctures to stave off the ailments of the women that sought her out for help.

She loved the different eras she lived through… watching as nations grew, and expanded, as cultures mingled and the enslaved became free. All the while knowing that eventually Death would pull her string and cut it off. For now, she was enjoying her freedom if that's what you could call it.

She still saw Death in her dreams. Sometimes it almost felt as if he was waiting for her to close her eyes. He would stalk her like a jungle cat would track its prey. He would corner her and say the most obscene things. He'd tell her what he wanted to do to her body. He would touch himself to tease her into wanting what she knew she could never take. If she gave into his manipulations, she would never be able to walk away. She'd always wake in a fevered sweat, tangled in her bedding, her body thrumming with desire.

If he was willing to torture her in her dreams, then she was going to take care of herself. Her hands snaked down her body to lift her nightdress, and she spread her legs as her fingers found her jewel. It was slick with her slippery juices as she began to circle it. She closed her eyes imagining it was Death's touch on her swollen bud, and her body tingled with her impending release. She couldn't deny to herself that she wanted him. She found herself thinking him more and more handsome as the years passed. He appeared to age at the same rate as her. Her back arched as she longed for his penetration to fill her empty well, to make her his woman after all these years. She cried out as her climax shuddered through her, "I love you!" She bit her tongue as penance for losing control once again leaving her soul as empty as her lady bits. She'd given in to his tormenting behavior again, "You bastard."

* * *

Death watched his female stir awake, she was oblivious to his presence. He was invisible to her eyes, and her lust made her senses blind to his nearness. He stood at the foot of the bed watching her desire for him unfold right before his eyes. He found the little noises she let escape her throat made his cock ache to hammer her sweet spot. The tension in his lower back tightened as he pictured himself feeding her hungry snatch his throbbing shaft. His hand slid inside his leather pants and curled around the base of his prick, and he stroked himself in rhythm with Vanessa's hips as they lifted and lowered from the bed. As she whimpered in ecstasy and raced to the edge of the cliff, his balls pulled up tight with his own need. He wished he could bury himself deep inside her wet walls and fill her with his seed. Her back arched, and she cried out, "I love you!" His heart went boom as he lost his load inside his pants. He'd bitten down on his lip too hard - he could taste his own blood, but he didn't care. She'd said she loved someone, and a sliver of anxiety ran through his core. Who did she love? He then heard her say, "You bastard." A sly smile lifted one corner of his lips as she answered his question for him. She was beginning to fall in love with him. If only she weren't such a stubborn woman, he would already have her by his side. Alas, he was not about to break his word by taking her against her will. 'That's fine. I'll wait forever for you my beloved,' he thought before he returned to his realm.

* * *

Vanessa held her breath as she felt the air around her shift. She punched the bed beside her, at the realization that he had been in the room with her. He'd witnessed the entire scene. She should have been embarrassed, but instead, she felt quite liberated. She smirked to herself knowing that she'd just taunted him. Well, she hoped he'd enjoyed the show because it would be the last one he got for a while. Tomorrow was a strong day for women of her abilities, and she had been practicing a couple of new charms and enchantments. She planned to vanish on the wind and with the right tools she could hide from him for a while – maybe even years if she was lucky. She yawned, then rolled over to find the sleep she needed to replenish her energy. The next day or two were going to be very draining.

CHAPTER 6

Death solidified in his bathroom. He waved his hand over his offending leathers that seemed to want to stick to his body in a disgusting manner. He smiled to himself because it had taken him many years to wear down his female's resistance and he was beginning see her to falter. He got the impression she was finally coming around to him.

He finished getting cleaned up in the shower, and with another wave of his hand, he was dry and redressed, ready to resume his list of collectibles for the day.

* * *

Vanessa rose early and gathered her cauldron, and a variety of herbs she'd collected over the last few days. She unfolded the piece of parchment and read over the list of things she needed. The last ingredient she required had to be collected fresh. She'd established an area where she could perform her ritual and only needed to place the last stone to complete the circle. She'd begun to bury the rocks when she'd arrived so they wouldn't be found by anyone but her. Along the last legs of her travels, she'd crossed paths with a fellow Druid and had exchanged herbs and recipes for a protection spell and a disappearing veil. She'd then set about putting everything in place waiting for the eclipse of the moon to happen. She would implore the goddess Luna to bid her doings with her blessing.

She bathed in a nearby stream, to cleanse her body, mind, and spirit. Then she made her way to her secluded location. Stepping between the doorways to her circle she removed the final stone from her sack and using her bare hands, began to dig into the earth. Once enough soil had been removed to bury the rock she started to chant under her breath as she covered it over.

MOTHER UNIVERSE HEAR MY CALL,
    I ask you to protect this ground,
    Come hell or high waterfall,
    May it never be found.

COSMO APPEARED IN THE SHADOWS watching the young witch Vanessa as she moved to the center of the protective boundary she'd completed. Cosmo recognized the redheaded beauty as her son's female when she turned her head to lay her hands on the small group of tools to her right. Cosmo sighed with disappointment. She had hoped that they would have sorted out their differences by now. She understood Death's need to have her come to him of her own free will. It was part of the law after all. Even though her children were Gods and Goddesses, they had to live by the rules she had put in place. For her to change things would be hypocritical.

Again Vanessa began to dig. She lifted the small tree she'd brought with her and planted its roots deep, filling in the hole around its base. She then removed the plug from the bladder of water amongst her supplies. She drew down the energy to pass through her body into the water as she watered the earth. She continued to recite the words from the parchment.....

Luna Lady of the night,
  Please grant me the gift of flight,
  The ability to move freely out of sight,

and placed gifts for the guardians of the forest around its base. A small jar of honey, a bladder of wine, a mix of various herbs and wildflowers. A bowl of sugar, one of fresh berries, she loosely tied three ribbons to the lower branches. Then finally she stood, satisfied with her offering. She completed the ritual by freeing the web weavers.

. . .

MAY THE WEB THEY WEAVE,
    Keep me from being seen.
* * *

Death was standing under the gallows. The man had been tried and found guilty of barbaric crimes against his neighbor. Death watched for the trapdoor to open and the man's body to fall at the end of a rope. He heard the henchman pull the lever, and he watched as Henry Stone's body bounced as the tension took up. Death observed as his collectibles dangled, kicking and fighting his binds, 'enough,' Death thought. Henry was a beast of a man, his sins too horrific to contemplate for any length of time. He positioned himself in front of the man's body, opened his mouth and began to inhale the dead man's soul. He made the process as painful as possible to forewarn Henry that life as he knew it was now well and truly over and there would be no second chances for him.

Fuck he hated the taste of the foul, putrid essence. It turned his stomach and made his head pound. The sooner he could unburden himself the better.

He staggered to the fiery pits of hell. This one would not see the Treasury of Souls, for it could be completely empty and he still would not release this man back into the fold. The bastard had slaughtered his neighbor and her entire family. He raced to the place of the condemned. With his hands on his knees, his stomach revolted, and with a cough, he spewed the corruption from his body into the care of his new keeper. Lucifer's right-hand man Leviathan said, "Welcome Henry Stone, to your new home. Make yourself comfortable. The fun starts shortly."

With a nod of his head toward Death, he threw a net over the latest prisoner, before vanishing with his new toy. Death shook his head and returned to his realm to shower and wash off the disgusting sensation on his skin.

After cleansing himself, he flopped backward on his bed naked and tried to reach out to his female. He needed the comfort of her calming soul, even if she were still pissed at him. He shot upright, his heart pounding against his ribs. He couldn't sense her... at all. The witch had somehow vanished off his radar. Fearful for his own sanity he screamed so loud the walls shook, "Vanessa!"

CHAPTER 7

Death had all but given up on ever finding Vanessa. His existence had returned to that of pre-Vanessa. He only slept to replenish his energy and kept his distance, for the most part, from his family. However, when he woke this time, he felt a shimmer roll throughout his realm. He held his breath as his heart rate kicked into top speed and his senses flared into overdrive. Something had changed; he could suddenly feel his female's essence. He rubbed his chest and wondered if she was aware the wards she'd put into place centuries ago had fallen. He wanted to race to her side and spank the succulent curve of her disobedient ass, but if she was unaware that her circumstances had changed, he didn't wish to tip his hand. He needed to use restraint, or he may lose her again, and that would be detrimental to the entire human realm. If anyone had touched what was rightfully his, he would kill them if they weren't already dead.

* * *

Vanessa woke slowly, stretched and checked the time. She lifted her phone up to her tired eyes, her alarm was set to go off in less than five minutes. She had a shift she needed to get ready for. She didn't feel like going to work today, but she had a patient on her floor that she was eager to follow up on. The old lady had no family to take care of her, and the other nurses weren't as sympathetic to the eighty-four-year-old dementia patient as she was. Her eighty-seven-year old sister Valmae had taken ill and wasn't able to visit that week.

Valmae had come by bus every day before being admitted to a hospital closer to her home. She used to bring clean clothes for a doll that Audrey carried around and babied as though it was real. Vanessa thought her harmless enough as long as you pampered to her delusions that the doll in Audrey's arms was her beautiful baby that needed to be bathed and changed into a new outfit for the day. Vanessa had stopped on the way home yesterday to buy an old-fashioned outfit from a second-hand store. She'd washed and dried the night before. She climbed out of bed and headed for the shower to get ready.

Her drive to work was uneventful; the only pleasure she got out of life was taking care of the lonely ones like Audrey. She placed her bag in her locker and pinned her tag to her chest. She had ten minutes before she had to start and she wanted to pop in on Audrey and give her the new outfit. By the time she did her rounds, Audrey would have forgotten that it was her that gifted it and think her sister had been for a visit.

As she entered the room, she picked up the baby doll that had been dropped beside the bed. She noted the monitors had been removed, and that Audrey looked peaceful in her sleep... too peaceful. Vanessa held the doll to her chest as she moved closer. Audrey's chest didn't rise and fall. "May your journey be blessed, lovely lady." She sat down hard in the chair next to the bed. She positioned Audrey's baby in the nook of her lifeless arm and held her hand. As a tear escaped her eye, the room shimmered. At first, she thought it was her watery eyes, but as she looked up, she was shocked to see Death standing on the other side of Audrey's bed. She froze, waiting to see whether he would notice her. Her heart skipped a beat when she acknowledged that a part of her wished he would.

"Audrey, it's time to go home to your baby. She waits for you in the treasury." Death spoke with respect for the old woman, and Vanessa felt herself softening her resolve to stay apart from him. He looked even more handsome than the last time she'd seen him. She watched Death lay a kiss on Audrey's forehead, then as he pulled away, he began to inhale through his mouth. Vanessa's eyes widened as she saw a beautiful white mist as it left Audrey's mouth and Death drew it in. Death stood upright, brushed the stray hair from Audrey's cheek and vanished right before her eyes.

He'd given no indication that he was aware she was even in the room.

Her heart felt heavy, and her soul felt lost. She wiped her tears away and headed for the nurse's station. Audrey's chart had a DNR on it, so she hadn't bothered to sound the alarms. She'd inform Sylvia shortly, but she wanted to prepare the body and make the call to Valmae to let her know her sister had passed. 'What a fucked up start to the day,' Vanessa thought.

* * *

Death released Audrey's soul into the treasury, then returned to the place he'd collected her from. He watched from a distance. Fuck he loved the way her hips swayed when she walked, and all he wanted to do was let her auburn waves loose from the tight bun she wore it in.

She seemed to be in a world all of her own as she went about her duties in a disciplined manner.

He couldn't stay any longer, or she might

discover him lurking about, so he returned to his duties with the intention of being back in time to follow her home.

* * *

Vanessa sat at the table in the staff cafeteria with her iPhone in one hand and a cup of coffee in the other. She'd put some thought into her current predicament during her shift and eventually worked out that something must have happened to the tree she'd planted all those years ago. She paused with her coffee cup halfway to her mouth to type in the search engine. As it did its thing she took a sip, you'd think after all these years she would be sick of the stuff, but she struggled to function without it. She almost spat it across the face of her phone as a picture of a leveled area came up on the screen. Local activists were currently lobbying against the construction company and developer over building a shopping mall. Her tree had been cut down... Fuck! That would explain why her wards had fallen and her spells had been broken. She narrowed her eyes and looked around the room, suddenly suspicious about her noninteraction with Death. She wondered if the bastard knew but just hadn't let on. She'd have to hand in her notice and look for another job. She should have known better than to get comfortable.

* * *

Death stopped by his eldest brother's realm to obtain his second volume of collectibles for the day. His brother's mood was odd, and he appeared to be somewhat anxious. When he pointed to the couch behind where Death stood his eyes followed his brother's finger. "Shit Bro, what the fuck have you done? Where did you take her from?"

Destiny snarled back at him as he moved closer to see what the young lady looked like. "Don't touch her." Death's hand dropped back to his side.

"Who is she?" Death asked curious about his brother's mental stability. He'd have to have a word with their mother about the situation if Destiny couldn't get a handle on his emotions.

After several minutes of confusing conversation with Destiny, he figured there wasn't much that happened that Cosmo didn't know about or have a hand in, so he bid his brother good luck and left to follow his own wayward woman.

* * *

Death materialized in the room of a teenage girl. He allowed her to see him as he spoke to her. "Young Tiffany you have fought the good fight for the sake of your family. It's time child." He leaned down and placed a kiss on her forehead. The door behind him opened, and he stilled with his eyes closed as he sensed Vanessa enter the room. Tiffany lifted her arms around Death's shoulders and whispered back, "I'm ready." She took a soft breath and licked her lips as she hugged him in fear. "Will it hurt?"

Death gave a slight shake of his head as he pulled back to look into Tiffany's eyes, "No child, your pain stops now. Take my hand, close your eyes and think of something you like to do more than anything else, then wish to do that in your next life." He began to inhale her soul as her arm slid from his shoulder to the bed and the monitors started to sound out the alarm.

Vanessa startled back to reality hitting the emergency call button and lowering the bed to begin CPR as was protocol. Even though Tiffany had undergone the last round of chemo a week ago, they found new branches of the disease spreading its arms far and wide throughout the girl's fragile body. She'd found Tiffany praying for death in the last couple of days when her mother and father weren't around. She'd told Vanessa, "I can't do this anymore, I just want it over," as she threw up into another bag.

The doctor entered the room and noted the time of death on Tiffany's chart, then asked if the girl's parents were around. Vanessa thought to herself his bedside manner was fucked up, and it wasn't the first time she'd thought that either. There was something about his mannerisms that made Vanessa think he should never have gone into the medical field. He was cheap and sleazy like a used car salesman.

Vanessa glanced at her watch, her shift finished two minutes ago, and she couldn't wait to get home and soak in a hot tub. She felt drained and was now looking forward to having a day off to sleep in and figure out what her next plan was.

Nurse Cindy walked into the room to begin her shift, and eager to leave, Vanessa did the hand over before heading to the locker room. She was exhausted from the day's events. It turned out to be one of her hardest shifts in a long time. As she left the hospital, she felt eyes watching her. Checking around, she saw one of the doctors waving at her. She quickly threw her hand up to wave back but didn't slow from heading in the direction of her car.

She didn't like Doctor Douchebag much either. She barely tolerated his presence when they had to work on the same shift. From gossip amongst the nurses, she'd heard he'd fuck anything in a nurse's uniform. 'All except me,' she thought. The idea of him touching her made her skin crawl. In fact, any man that touched her made her feel like her nerve endings were being zapped by electricity, causing her pain. It was like her body rebelled against anyone getting close, in all the time since casting her spells and putting her wards in place. Even just a tap on the shoulder from someone in passing was enough to cause significant discomfort, and her brand would ignite to remind her that her body belonged to Death.

She parked her car in the garage and walked up the steps to her apartment. As she put the key into the lock, she looked over her shoulder again. With a sigh she unlocked it and entered, toeing off her shoes just inside the door before shutting and locking it again.

* * *

Death had followed Vanessa from the hospital. It was convenient that one of the doctors happened to be standing outside waving. He allowed her to put a little distance between them as she drove out of the carpark. He followed her progression towards her home. He thought he'd given himself away as she paused at her front door before he vanished back to his realm.

CHAPTER 8

Vanessa had soaked in the hot tub until her fingers and toes looked like shriveled up prunes. Her tired, aching muscles had relaxed enough so she would be finally able to sleep. She was looking forward to having a sleep in for a change, but as she turned her phone to silent on the nightstand, she saw she'd missed a call and two text messages. With a sigh, she returned the call to her supervisor and said, "Hi Sharon, I missed a call and a couple of texts." She yawned as she climbed in-between her sheets naked.

"I know I'm asking more than I should

Vanessa, but I've got three called in sick with stomach flu. Is there any chance you can work? I don't want to bring in agency staff if I can help it. You know, that's just a drama, and I don't feel up for potluck," Sharon begged.

"Fine, what time? I'll need to set the alarm," Vanessa asked with another yawn. She always figured she could sleep when she was dead, then laughed at her own unspoken joke.

"Can you be here to replace Lisa? She was supposed to start at 5:30am. Thanks, hon, love your guts!" Sharon hung up before Vanessa could respond or complain about the ridiculous start time. Within seconds of setting her alarm and turning off the light, she was out cold.

* * *

Lucifer entered his throne room to find Leviathan whispering to Ezekiel. "Why are you not in the chamber of souls, Zeak? Is there something I should be aware of boy?"

"No my Lord," Ezekiel replied, knowing that the term he used for a higher god was just as derogatory as Lucifer calling him 'boy.' Z was quite happy to wait for the bitch slap which took place instantly. He hit the brimstone inside the chamber he was supposed to be working in.

"Fuck you asshole," he cursed as he lifted his crumpled body from the scorching hot rock. "I will reap vengeance one day soon you cunt struck pussy." As if Lucifer had heard his words, his feet were lifted off the floor of the cavern, and his back was pressed against the molten lava covered walls.

Leviathan materialized with his hand clasped around Ezekiel's throat. He snarled in his ear, "Don't tempt him you fool. I have worked too long and too hard to earn his respect and my place. Our plan is in motion. For once in your pathetic existence be fucking patient my friend or I will serve your intestines to the hounds, again."

* * *

Death watched from a distance as Vanessa left for work, then materialized inside her bedroom. The area was kept neat and tidy, and with a sigh of relief, he noted there were no signs to indicate that a man had ever been there. In fact, he noticed that apart from a handful of necessary items the place was quite bare, void of personal attachments. On examining all the rooms, he found the same sparse accompaniments. The only thing that stood out was an altar, set up with a small cauldron, candles, herbs, and charms. On lifting the edge of the cloth coverings, he saw the spine of what looked like an ancient leather-bound journal. As his fingers reached out to stroke its surface, it zapped his fingertips with its power. He smirked at his beloved, "Little witch, still evading my touch I see." Although he knew the protection of her spells was not aimed at him, he still took it personally.

He pondered for a moment whether she would seek him out if he were to capture the book and take it to his realm. She would undoubtedly know it was him that had taken it. "Not this time my love, but maybe another," he decidedly vocalized. With that, he vanished to be on time for his next assignment. He conceded that by now his woman would surely know he was coming for her. "Let the games begin sweetheart. I'm playing for keeps this time."

* * *

Vanessa knew that the wards being down meant that she and Death would begin to play a cat-and-mouse game again. The thought was not all that frightening to her anymore. She'd always found him attractive, and just the simple thought of him touching her or kissing her would ignite her hormones. Her appetite for him had been on hiatus, and the mere sight of him would keep her in wet dreams for another six months. She needed to hand in her notice and move on to another location. As she sat at the table in the cafeteria eating her lunch, she glanced at her phone searching the vacancies. She quickly submitted emails of interest along with her work history to a couple of them not far from her present location, but far enough away that it would mess with Death's inner compass when trying to find her. It would give her enough time to find another place to stay as well as install some barriers and mirrors to deflect him. She rang Sharon and explained that a family emergency had come up and that she would have to leave as soon as she finished her shift in an hour and a half. Then she sent a letter of resignation to both Sharon and the payroll officer. The rest of her shift flew by without any further drama. She said a quick goodbye to the other nurses as they did the changeover and raced home to throw everything into her car. She would stay in a hotel tonight and begin to look for a new month to month in the morning.

With her car packed and loaded with a handful of boxes, she surveyed the street before pulling out of the driveway. She'd spoken to the local real estate about having to vacate the premises and left the key in an envelope on the kitchen table. She'd explained that an abusive ex-boyfriend had been spotted in the area and that she had to move on quickly. The estate agent had sympathized and said that if she needed a tenant's reference to contact her directly so there wouldn't be a paper trail. In a little under an hour's travel, she had reached her next destination. She'd driven around in circles for the first ten minutes to ensure she wasn't being followed. As she slid from the driver's seat, she focused all her energy and sent it out to see if it bumped into a certain man or god that she was praying was otherwise too occupied to notice that she had done another vanishing act. She laughed to herself again muttering under her breath, "Catch me if you can baby." With a sigh, she turned to the office of the motel and walked up to the clerk. "One room, one night. Cash." She filled out the paperwork and offered a flash of her driver's license. At least it would be safe and comfortable for the night. She would fire up her laptop and see what she could find as soon as she had a hot shower and got out of her work uniform.

* * *

Death stood at the door to cell block B, the guards had turned their backs and walked away leaving the door to Lance Henry's cage unlocked. He leaned against the bars waiting for the job to be done. Connor O'Grady had walked into Lance's space and got up in the inmate's face, before palming the toothbrush he'd sharpened into a pick. Connor thrust it several times into Lance's gut before finally snapping it off and walking away. Connor returned to his own cage three cells down, washed his hands and flushed the remnants of the weapon down his toilet. He looked over his shoulder, and with a nod of his head, he confirmed with an Irish roll of his tongue, "It's done. The motherfucker's as good as dead."

Death stepped closer while Lance Henry struggled to suck in his last breaths. His lung collapsed, and he began to drown in his own blood. Death knelt down beside the dying man, "Lance Henry, you reap what you sow. You'll not pass lightly from this life to the afterlife or to the next. Even if the treasury of souls were to be empty, I would not release you from the pits of hell." Death pressed his lips to the putrid man's forehead, knowing this one would be hard to contain until he made its delivery. The thought of having such a depraved soul inside of his body triggered his gag reflex. He snarled in contempt of his duties. Lance Henry's body began to tremble in fear, or maybe it was the loss of blood making him feel chilled. Death didn't really care, he had no sympathy for rock spiders. He had been found guilty of sixteen counts of rape involving minors. Death began to inhale through his teeth, he imagined his teeth to be as sharp as razor blades. He stood and swayed as he regained his composure, trying not to choke on the rankness of the man's soul burning his throat. He vanished instantly and landed on his knees in front of Lucifer, his hands on the ground in front of him, and he began to cough. Lucifer frowned, "Are you, alright son?" He hadn't seen Death look so affected by a collection in quite some time, although he probably had been handing more of his duties over to Leviathan lately. His heart just wasn't in it anymore. At first, he'd been forced to do it as punishment for coveting what his creator had but didn't want. Then he'd done it purely to defy his creator, as it was his right to do, he scorned the one that had scorned him. Now he was miserable. He was constantly in a foul mood and had zero tolerance for taking care of what he'd been put in charge of. The only person he seemed to desire any interaction with was Death, the second eldest son of his beloved Cosmo. He slapped the young god of death on the back, and with the force to cough up a lung, Death spewed the feral soul forth from his gut. He wiped his lips and waved his hand at Lucifer, "This one deserves your worst."

Lucifer nodded his head, "As you wish." He stuck two fingers between his lips and whistled. Leviathan appeared before the sound had ended reverberating around the rock walls, threw a stinging net over the soul then disappeared into the pit of the damned.

Death vanished with his arm wrapped around his waist, his muscles shivering and twitching from the burden of being contaminated by such filth. He disintegrated his clothing and landed in his bathroom, swaying as he used his mind to turn the water on. He then staggered underneath to slide down the tiles to rest his ass on the floor, his elbows on his bent knees and his head in his hands. He didn't know how much longer he could continue to do this shit. He needed his Vanessa to put him back together again, to make him feel alive and whole before there was nothing left of his sanity to offer.

CHAPTER 9

Vanessa stayed an extra night in the hotel while she went about having the power and gas transferred from her old address to her new one. She had managed to find an adequate apartment that was set up for a month-to-month. She'd paid the two months in advance and was due to move in the following day. The condo was fully furnished so that only left a spot of grocery shopping in the morning before moving in. She jumped in the shower to get ready to go out for dinner, feeling right about her day. As she washed the shampoo from her hair, her head began to swirl. She became dizzy, and her chest ached. In all the years she had been alive she'd never experienced a sensation of wrongness so strongly. Her knees buckled, and she found herself unable to brace against the darkness threatening to take her down to the tiles. Her instant reaction was to panic as she waited for the impact. It didn't come; instead, she felt the warmth of a hard body below her, and she opened her eyes in confusion searching for what had broken her fall. She gasped when she recognized the crumpled pile of limbs below her. She lifted her head to see she was no longer in the motel's shower but another.

What the fuck was going on? She didn't understand how she'd come to be in this strange place with the man who claimed to be her husband. But regardless of how, Vanessa knew at a glance that he needed her help. She took a deep breath and using the wall, she lifted herself up off him, but he didn't move. He appeared to be unconscious or at least too weak to put up much of a fight. Her heart went out to the man that she knew was supposed to be infallible, yet, here right now, he looked worse than death.

When she reached out to touch his forehead, she felt an oily substance covering his skin, and it left her feeling cold and repulsed. She wasn't sure what it was, but instinct told her the stuff needed to be washed off. Vanessa reached out for the washcloth scrunched in her man's hand then looked around for the soap. She found a large bottle on a shelf built into the wall of the shower. Soaping up the cloth she began to scour every inch of his skin to remove the greasy coating. She washed his hair then lifted the shower-rose off the wall and hosed him off, trying not to drown him in the process. She quickly cleaned herself to ensure that none of the contaminating substance had made it onto her skin, then turning the shower off, she stepped out and snatched up a towel for each of them. After wrapping herself in one, she squatted down beside Death and lifted his head to face her. Her heart broke for him seeing him so vulnerable and broken, the words falling from her lips before she could censor her brain, "Baby, help me. I can't carry you on my own. You need to try to stand up."

Death opened his eyes to find himself hallucinating. His Vanessa was there wrapped in a fluffy white towel. He smirked as his eyes followed the length from her knee up under the gaping fabric to her neatly trimmed snatch. Fuck, he ached all over, and he didn't particularly like the tiles cutting into his ass cheek either. With his eyes beginning to close again from exhaustion, all he could think was that he wished he was in bed curled up with his beautiful redheaded angel. He could hear his hallucination saying something to him, but wasn't able to focus his thoughts enough to comprehend the waffled words. 'Did she call me baby?' His brain stuck on that one word and kept replaying it over and over in his mind.

Vanessa panicked as she saw his eyes start to close again, "Sweetie stay with me… Can you open your eyes for me, baby?" With a squeak, she fell sideways, and Death curled around her body effectively trapping her in place on his massive bed. Vanessa froze, holding her breath, as Death brushed his lips against the nape of her neck and moaned. He threw his leg over hers as he pulled her back closer to his body. Vanessa bit her lower lip as desire flooded her system like a match to dry tinder. Her hips involuntarily rolled her terry covered ass toward his already thickened member. She found herself barely able to refrain from groaning with need as he made the fabric between them disappear. She began to pant, her body so on fire for his touch. She was certain she would self-combust if he didn't let her go. She needed to get out before she allowed him to take her, even in his present state. If she didn't get out, she didn't know if she would be able to resist touching him. For no love or money could she deny the truth of the fact that this man owned her soul? It would seem he was the only man that could touch her without causing her pain unless you counted the extreme pleasure of his touch that at the moment was making her body ache with unsatisfied arousal. As she stiffened her back to make an attempt to leave his bed, he snarled beside her ear. "Can you not just let me have my beloved in my dreams for one night? I vow I will release her heart on my waking until she comes to me of her own free will."

Vanessa realized then that Death thought her to be a dream, a figment of his damaged imagination. In this place, wherever she was, his word was law. He could not break it without suffering immensely, for that alone she surrendered to his plea and shifted to see his handsome face. With a hand cupping each side of his face, Vanessa ran her thumb across his bottom lip. "Shhh, my love, calm yourself. I am here for tonight only, provided I have your word that you will release me when I wake." With his eyes still closed he licked his lips, and as his tongue brushed Vanessa's thumb, his eyes opened wide. He swiftly rolled Vanessa onto her back caging her beneath him. "Is this some sort of witch trick my beloved has designed to drive me even more mad than I already am?" Vanessa refused to show fear. Instead, she lifted her head from the mattress, brushing his lips against hers. Death stiffened unsure what to make of what was unfolding before him.

Death was so besotted with his beautiful

redheaded witch that his resistance came crashing down around his heart. Her tongue slid along the seam of his hard-set mouth. When he didn't open for her, she slid her hands up into his hair and nipped his lower lip. She lifted her legs to hook her ankles behind his back and his mouth opened in a groan. Vanessa teased him with her tongue, deepening the kiss, dominating his body from her submissive position. She coaxed him into taking control of his desire. If he was going to let her go in the morning, then she wanted to finally know what the kiss of Death would really be like. He surrendered to the moment and returned her passion. He felt his body surge with power and energy rejuvenating his weary soul. It was like he'd just been struck by lightning and his entire body hummed with electricity. In the midst of sensory overload the head of his throbbing cock aligned with Vanessa slippery pussy. Death lowered himself to his elbows to anchor himself and curled his hands under Vanessa's shoulders to hold her in place. Then with one fast hard roll of his hips, he impaled himself fully inside his wife. Death swallowed Vanessa's cry as he broke her virginal barrier. "Shhh, it's done baby," he cooed, kissing away a tear as it escaped her closed eyes. "Look at me, angel. Open your eyes and look at me." He waited for her to do as he said, holding perfectly still, he allowed her body to relax beneath him. As she slowly opened her eyes, he slid out of her body to the tip, then slowly he worked his way back inside. He kept eye contact with Vanessa's green eyes the entire time, knowing that he was not just teaching her body of his love for her, but also her soul. This time when he sank his full length inside of her, he felt her acceptance, her muscles tightened around him in a small contraction. Vanessa bit her lip and nodded her head to indicate she liked what he was doing. She didn't trust her voice, her throat was dry and felt as though it was on fire. Her breathing became heavy, and her hands lowered to his back where she dug her nails in when the sensations became so intense she thought she would faint.

Death rolled his hips to apply just the

right pressure to Vanessa's G-spot with the head of his length and her clit with his pelvic bone at the same time. Vanessa's back arched and her heels dug into Death's lower back when her climax hit, he finally claimed his wife. As her inner muscles milked his shaft, Death roared loudly with his own orgasm, spilling his seed deep inside Vanessa's fertile womb. He rolled them sideways still buried inside his woman and kissed her. He wanted to ask her to stay with him but knew she wouldn't.

CHAPTER 10

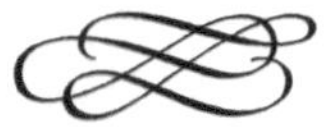

Death woke to find he was alone. Only the sticky residue and the smell of sex on the sheets told him that last night hadn't been a dream. He turned over and cuddled the pillow to his chest; it still held the warmth of his wife's head, she must have only just left. His hand slid across the mattress to try to capture her essence. His hand met with the damp spot from their coupling, and he opened his eyes to find the evidence of his claim - a smeared confirmation that even when cloaked she had stayed faithful to him by not taking a lover. He'd waited much too long to have her, but did it mean he would have to be well and truly broken before she would come to his side again?

With a sigh he threw back the sheet and crawled out of bed, wistfully wishing that his female was still there to keep his mind and body busy. For the first time in a long time, he actually felt hungry. Usually, he didn't eat food, it wasn't like he would starve to death if he didn't eat. The non-necessary substance never sat well when he was collecting the deceased souls that seemed to be finding their way onto his list more and more every day.

* * *

Vanessa woke naked in her motel bed, the sheets twisted and tangled. She sat up and looked around to see if she was alone. As she shifted her legs to the edge of the bed preparing to stand, she noted the dry smear of her broken virginity on the inside of her thigh. She fell back on the bed, "What have I done?" she cursed at herself for not being able to resist him. Not wanting to think about what she'd allowed to happen, she checked the time and raced for the shower. She had too many things to take care of today, and if she was going to stay under her husband's radar, then she needed to get a move on. First up she had an appointment to see a man about a bike, she'd made a booking to take the new Kawasaki Ninja for a ride, even though she'd already decided she was going to buy it.

* * *

Death arrived back in his realm. He was furious with Vanessa. The little witch had done a runner again. He'd also noticed that while in-between her thighs the night before that she wasn't wearing the amulet he'd given her centuries ago. And to make matters worse, she'd had a tattoo done over the top of his mark. He would spank her ass for her blatant rejection of him as her husband. When Vanessa had first tied herself to him, he'd spent months in Destiny's library trying to find her book. However, it was forever elusive, if it existed at all. He sometimes pondered as to whether his mother knew more than she let on. With the simple thought of Cosmo, the air around him shifted. "Fuck me!" he growled, before turning to find her standing in the middle of the room.

"That's no way to greet your mother," she said snidely.

Death faced off against Cosmo, "Now is not a good time mother. Can we do this later?" He was thinking maybe the twelfth of never sounded good to him. He wanted to start looking for Vanessa before she had too much of a head start. She'd obviously already planned on moving, as her place was empty when he went there. He knew she was good but not good enough to be gone in under half an hour.

Cosmo dug her heels in, "No. You know this is inevitable. You must go now, it's time. I'm not going to stand here and argue about this."

Death suddenly saw his mother in a new light. She gave the humans free will but refused to offer it to him. "Fine, I'll do it. Not like I ever have a choice." He closed his eyes, thinking of Vanessa and vanished.

When Death opened his eyes next, he found himself in a hospital bed, his chest felt heavy, and he could barely get enough air into his lungs to breathe. He had tubes up his nose, drips attached to his wrist, and he tried to lift his head off the pillow so he could check under the bed covering. 'You've gone too fucking far this time Mother.' He cursed with the recognition that he was, in fact, pissing into a bag through a tube. She was never going to give him a break, was she? At the worst, it would be seven days of being bedridden. As he swore at his mother and her shittier than now timing, a thought came to mind. Where exactly was he? Before he could ponder the question much longer, the monitors began to sound alarms, and he blacked out.

* * *

Vanessa pulled up at her new apartment. Fuck she loved the purr of the motor between her legs. She hadn't had an adrenalin rush like it in a long time. She removed her helmet and shook out her long auburn curls and smiled to herself, thinking if she'd known sex would make her feel so alive and so damn sexy, she laughed. "I so would have done it centuries ago."

Scotty, the new owner of her car,

climbed from behind the wheel after following her. "Are you sure you don't want to keep it, she's a beauty," he said running his hand over the hood.

"I'm sure, I just need my stuff out of the trunk, and she's all yours." Vanessa smiled, heading to open the front door to her new place. She clipped it back and returned to retrieve her belongings from the trunk. After everything was inside, she waved him off, eager to venture around her new residence. She found the perfect spot to set up her altar and as she finished, there was a knock at the door, "Who is it?" she called out walking toward it.

"Home delivery," a young male voice answered before she opened the door. He unloaded his van, grabbed a quick signature and left. Vanessa was keen to see him go, she didn't like the way he looked around every time he'd returned to the van for another load. There was also something creepy about the way he scrutinized her chest. Once he was gone, she unzipped her leather jacket and placed it on the back of the couch. She packed the freezer with a handful of microwave dinners and a couple of loaves of bread, blessing the person who owned the apartment for having to move to the UK on short notice due to work commitments for the next twelve months. Once the groceries were packed away, and she'd opened and closed every drawer and cupboard in the kitchen, she moved to the lounge room. Rubbing her hands together in glee, she turned on the stereo. "This feels right," she said to the walls with a smile. Her phone rang in her jacket, and she reached into the pocket to answer it pulling out the contents.

"Hello," she took the call not familiar with the number.

"Hi is this Vanessa Mc Duffie?" the male voice on the other end inquired.

Unsure of who was asking, Vanessa's voice took on the Irish lilt of her past, "Cana be axing who might be calling? She jus' be away from the phone right now."

"This is Dominic De Silver, I'm the director of nursing at Saint Andrew's. Could you ask Vanessa to give me a call as soon as she returns? She can reach me at this number."

"Just a moment sir, she's just walked in." Vanessa shuffled the phone from one hand to the other, cleared her throat and said, "Hello, this is Vanessa."

"My name is Dominic DeSilver. Your agency said that you were looking for a full-time nursing placement. You come highly recommended. Would you be available later today to take a tour of the hospital and fill out the necessary paperwork?"

"I can be there in an hour and a half, is that suitable?"

"Perfect, I look forward to meeting you. Just go to the reception area, and they will notify me of your arrival."

Vanessa ended the call, then danced her way to the bedroom. She yawned, eyeing off the queen-size bed. She pointed at the mattress and said, "Later! Stop looking at me like that. You know I'm weak-willed when it comes to pillow-tops." She spun on her heal and ignored its appeal.

CHAPTER 11

Vanessa reported to the reception desk at Saint Andrew's to meet Mister De' Silver. She took a seat, balancing her helmet on her knee and waited for him to appear. Within a few minutes the door of the elevator opened and a tall gentleman somewhere in his late thirties walked out with a smile in place. He reached out his hand, "Welcome to our hospital. I'm Dominic De Silver." He glanced at his watch then added, "How about we start with the tour and wind it up with the paperwork in my office?" Vanessa briefly shook his hand after bracing herself for the bite of discomfort. It was only mild, much less than usual, 'That's odd,' she thought.

"This way Miss McDuffie," he said directing her to the elevator he'd walked out of only minutes before. "Because of your qualifications and your employer's recommendations, I have assigned you to work in the Intensive Care Unit. I believe that's as good as any place to begin your tour."

When the lift dinged to indicate they had reached the fourth floor, Vanessa's stomach fluttered, her power sparked, and her hand instinctively reached into her pocket to feel for the charm that seemed to calm her when it rested in her palm. Not finding it she checked the other pockets, the memory of her emptying them when her phone rang earlier. Her carelessness left her agitated when Dominic's hand touched her elbow to direct her out of the elevator.

* * *

Leviathan called to Ezekiel, "It is time," he smiled showing his jagged sharp teeth. His hand cupped the back of Ezekiel's skull, the palm of his right hand pressed to his forehead and with an explosion of pain

Ezekiel's essence was set free. Leviathan lowered Ezekiel's body to the floor of the cave and covered it with rocks to hide its location. Each of the stones had a symbol painted on them in Lucifer's blood. Leviathan had stolen it drop by precious drop over the past century. He had dried it into a powder, then when the time was growing near, he'd reconstituted it with his own and Ezekiel's blood. They had both painstakingly painted the elements onto the rocks until there were enough to cover the body of Ezekiel while he ventured forth into the human realm.

Dominic swayed beside Vanessa and hissed, lifting his hand to his temple. He shook it as though he suddenly felt dizzy. "Are you alright? You look a little pale."

Dominic felt as though his throat were scorched and he could smell ash in his sinuses. He coughed to clear his chest and then Dominic was gone. Ezekiel overshadowed the spirit of the man he possessed, pushing him into the crazy corner of his mind. Ezekiel stretched inside the body, then noticed a beautiful female standing next to him. "Oh, yes I'm fine. I just remembered something I forgot to do earlier. Now, where were we?"

Vanessa frowned not feeling comfortable with the shift in Dominic's energy. She didn't know the man, but he suddenly seemed different. "You were about to show me the ICU ward, where I'll be working."

"Yes, yes that's right. This way," he said, following the arrowed signs.

When they moved to the last room with a patient, Vanessa could have sworn she saw a flare of burnt orange radiate through Dominic's brown eyes. But that was completely offset by the recognition of the man lying in the hospital bed on the other side of the glass wall in front of her.

Her limbs had gone numb, her lips were moving, and words were being said, and before she knew what she was doing, she'd told Dominic, "I rescind my application, I can't work here." With feet made of lead encased in concrete boots and a mind of their own they had her moving towards Death.

Dominic's hand on her shoulder made

her jump, startling her back to reality. "You can't go in there. Family members only."

Vanessa looked at the man in the bed then back at Dominic and informed him in a voice scant above a whisper, "I am family, he's my husband."

Ezekiel froze, "If he is your husband then… what is his name?" he inwardly smirked, ecstatic with hearing the news. The woman could be used as leverage in the grand scheme of things. It was perfect.

"He is Reaper, Reaper McDuffie," she ad-libbed, looking back at the patient in the bed.

"You will be required to sign in at the nurse's station so that you may visit with him," Ezekiel instructed.

Vanessa did as she'd been told then entered Death's room. She sat in a chair beside the bed after brushing a kiss to his brow. Restless she stood and took the chart from the foot of the bed and started to read it. She moved the chair closer to the bed, lowered the rail and leaned her head on her arms and closed her eyes, listening to the shallow breaths and the beeping monitors.

* * *

Ezekiel stood in the shadows watching Vanessa, the familiarity in which she moved around Death's human form, intrigued him no end. He studied her for several minutes finding her fascinating, making him curious to investigate how this marriage had come about. 'Maybe later' he thought,' I have a week to get everything I need. Time to have a little fun methinks.' He headed for the elevators, slapping the ass of a blonde nurse as he passed. He filtered through the memories of the man's body he'd abducted. He didn't bother to return to the guy's office. He went down to the ground floor, walked past the reception area and out the front door. He paused momentarily, looking around at the all you can eat smorgasbord the world had to offer. Lifting his arms out to his sides, he snarled to no-one in particular. "It's good to be alive."

* * *

Death opened his eyes, certain he was dreaming. His hand rested on the silken red curls of his Vanessa's head. His hand involuntarily twitched, and it slid free of her hair as her head rose and her eyes fluttered open to meet his gaze. "Hey, my beautiful angel, what are you doing here?" he struggled to say the words, with insufficient air in his lungs. Vanessa slid her hand inside his trying to hide her tears from his view.

"I don't understand, what are you doing here?" she asked, confused as to why a god would be in a hospital bed and according to the chart she'd read… dying. The man before her was in desperate need of a heart-lung transplant and to complicate the situation he had pneumonia. Her chest ached for the man who was her soul mate. "Why is this happening? What can I do?"

"It is a long story, and it began thousands of years ago, long before I met you," he explained.

CHAPTER 12

Ezekiel walked into the strip club, pulled out the wallet from his back pocket and paid the cover charge. Taking a seat in the front row, he waved down the topless waitress, "We have a two drinks minimum and a two drinks maximum sir, what would you like."

Ezekiel smiled, "I'll have two double whiskeys." He presented her with a hundred-dollar bill and stopped her from arguing by telling her to keep the change.

The curtain separated at the back of the stage, and a skinny woman with long blonde hair came onto the scene, "Eat a fucking burger," he said into the glass the waitress had delivered, throwing back the entire contents. The phone in the inside pocket of his jacket began to ring for the third time. He retrieved it and looked at the screen, then sifted through the man's mind to identify the name attached to the caller. "Miss Wendy," he answered.

"Dominic? Are you alright? I rang your office, and they said you'd just walked out. Everyone's worried." Wendy's voice seemed to display concern for her fiancé's whereabouts.

"I'm just peachy," Ezekiel replied.

"Dominic, have you been drinking? Sweetheart tell me where you are. I'll come and get you. We'll find a meeting somewhere. I don't know what's happened, but you were doing so well."

After referencing information in the man's memory, Ezekiel worked out the man, Dominic was a dry drunk. Wendy was his fiancé, and because he had a drinking problem they hadn't slept together in the twelve months they had been dating. "So

Wendy, if I tell you where I am, are you going to let me fuck you?" he asked, already knowing the answer from her gasp. "Yeah, didn't think so. I tell you what, you can go fuck yourself, and while you're down on your knees praying for my soul, you can open your mouth wide and suck the good Lord's cock." He hung up on her as she began to pray. He switched the phone off and lifted his eyes back to the stage, to see the blonde with no shape leave the stage.

The guy at the table next to him lit up a cigarette, and Ezekiel tilted his head in the man's direction. "Do you have a spare?" The man leaned over and offered him one, flipping open his Zippo lighter. Ezekiel stared at the flame, tempted to throw his second glass of whiskey over it. The man whistled at him to get his attention, "Do you want a light or not?" Ezekiel shook his head, eyeing off the matchbook sitting in the ashtray. He picked it up, flipped it open and struck a match, inhaling the smell of sulfur before lighting his tailor-made. Sucking in a big drag of smoke he blew out the flame again enjoying the smell of the afterburn of a lit match. He slipped the matchbook into his pocket for later, just in case he got homesick.

* * *

Vanessa was pissed on Death's behalf. What kind of mother does this sort of thing to her son? To set him up to spend a miserable week on Earth after which he wound up dead anyway. She found herself unable to leave him alone. It had taken all his energy to explain what he'd been through over his many lives on Earth. With every new tale, he claimed another small fragment of the heart that she knew already belonged to him.

Over the duration of five days, she had told him stories of her travels, the people she'd met and those that had influenced her life. She gave him sponge baths which caused him to bemoan his bedridden state.

Vanessa discovered that she would give anything to put an end to his suffering. She watched him sleeping peacefully, then with a sigh she stood and made her way to the coffee machine next to the nurse's station.

She pulled out some money and fed it into the machine, then began pressing buttons. A woman appeared beside her from nowhere. She collected her cup from the dispenser and shifted out of the woman's way. "Sorry," she apologized as the woman stepped sideways to block her exit. Vanessa frowned, lifting her eyes from her cup, waiting for the woman to move around her. She squinted, there was something really familiar about the woman's presence.

Her eyes grew wide as the woman addressed her as though she knew her well. "Finally we meet face-to-face Vanessa." She waved her hand towards a row of chairs to the side. "We have much to discuss, you and I. Shall we?"

Vanessa moved her free hand to the base of the cup to prevent her from losing her grip, then slowly walked to the sitting area.

"Let me tell you a story. There was once a young man who, at the age of twenty-one, took over the duties of his mother, as all her children had done when they were ready. The mother never wanted her son to ever forget what it was like to die and commanded that he live a human life for up to a week at a time when she was fit to maintain his role as the reaper of souls. On one such visit many centuries ago, he stumbled upon a young maiden who had lost her family to a vicious plague. She cared for him as was in her nature as a healer to do. However, the young woman's despair drove her to slice her palm with a dagger and place the open wound against that of the diseased and dying man. Unbeknownst to the young witch, she had, in her actions, tied her life to that of a god. Now, even in the fevered state of the god's human form, he remembered the redheaded angel who showed him compassion and cared for him in his hour of need. He began to dream of this woman until his desire for her started to affect his mind." She paused looking at the coffee cup in Vanessa's hand, "You should drink that before it goes cold, instead of just staring at it. There's nothing worse than a cold cup of coffee."

"Now where was I? Oh yes, the young woman woke to find that she was in perfect health, and with total disregard for her own life and virtue, decides to travel the world." She waved her hand dismissively. "The young maiden, on discovering her action in creating a blood tie to the god of death, tried to run from her husband at every possible chance she could find. Until one night when the eclipse of the moon was in perfect alignment, the young witch Vanessa cast a powerful combination of spells effectively hiding herself away from the husband that would forever seek the company of his wife. You have been involved with my family for a very long time. My son has a good heart, and he does not take his duties lightly, but your words prevented me from helping him when you cast your spells that day. Those wards were broken when your tree and circle were destroyed. I think my son is a romantic fool, allowing you to avoid taking your rightful place at his side. More to the point my dear daughter-in-law, I heard your plea. You said you would give anything to make his suffering stop. What would you do if I told you that you could indeed put an end to his suffering?"

Vanessa let out the breath she'd been

holding as she drained the last of her coffee, then straightened her spine with Irish iron, though when she spoke it was barely a frightened whisper. "Anything."

Cosmo placed a hand on Vanessa's arm, "Good, here's what's going to happen."

CHAPTER 13

Ezekiel wrapped his hand around the young, blonde nurse's hair, clenching it in his fist as he pumped his hips back and forth. He was so engrossed in fucking the woman that he didn't hear the front door open. Asmodeus leaned his shoulder against the door jamb, as he watched the demon spend the human's seed inside the willing woman. "Are you quite done Zeak?" he asked in a deep, gravelly voice.

"Aargh! I wondered how long before one of you fuckers would find me," he said, sliding his softening cock free of the woman. With a slap to her ass, he added, "Get out."

"As you wish, but I will be sending you back to hell before I leave," Asmodeus responded.

"Not you, fallen," he snarled, looking at the blonde as she lay on the bed. "I meant her." He waved his hand to indicate the disposable fuck.

"Miss I strongly suggest you get up, get dressed and leave now while you still can," Asmodeus told the young nurse. She sobbed as she scampered off the bed and snatched up her clothes.

"Will you call me?" she asked looking at the floor.

"Not likely," Ezekiel answered before turning his back on her as he walked into the bathroom.

Asmodeus watched the woman's body tremble as she dressed herself. She walked toward him then paused as he shifted to block her only means of exit. He reached out his hand to cup her face, "You will go straight to the pharmacy and purchase the morning after pill. You will take that tablet before you climb in your car to venture home. When you arrive home, you will shower and climb into bed as though none of this ever happened. You never came here, you never saw the inside of this apartment, and you never fucked that beast. If you do remember any fragments, they are simply pieces of a dream you had a few nights ago, an insignificant event that is a figment of your imagination. He exhaled a breath in her face with a puff. She blinked a couple of times, shook her head and moved past him to the front door letting herself out. Asmodeus entered the bathroom to find Ezekiel in the shower.

"So demon, what brings you to Middle Earth and does your father know you are here?" As one of the fallen, Asmodeus had grown quite territorial over the millenniums. He was still ruled by his guilty charge 'Lust' as judged by his maker. At first, he had been vengeful at being sentenced to spend eternity in Middle Earth. But thousands of years later, men and women alike worshipped him, as they all lusted after something or someone.

"My visit is but part of a plan," Ezekiel

admitted, knowing that Asmodeus and his lust for information would be peaked.

"I'm listening," Asmodeus shifted his weight and folded his arms over his chest, unaware that he'd just confirmed Ezekiel's thoughts with his actions.

Ezekiel tilted his head back under the spray to hide his smirk of victory. 'One down, six to go,' he thought.

* * *

Cosmo collapsed at the foot of Lucifer's throne, her body shaking and covered in an oily residue. She coughed and clawed at her throat as she released the diseased soul of the murderer she had just collected. Lucifer called for Leviathan to retrieve the new prisoner. "Take her away, flay her for her sins, and then as she begs, heal her and flay her again for taking the lives of your innocent children. I charge her with the worst punishments we have to offer. Now leave us be."

With a nod of his head, Leviathan glanced sideways at the crumpled form of Cosmo. He captured the evil soul and vanished to partake in delivering its judgment, all the while smiling to himself at how well everything was coming together. He was manifesting his own brand of divine intervention, and Lucifer was utterly oblivious to what was going on around him.

Lucifer bent down and scooped his beloved Cosmo up into his arms, "My goddess, why do you torture us this way? Let me take care of you, I beg you. It breaks me to see you like this." On hearing no arguments from his love, he carried her to his bed.

* * *

Vanessa returned to Death's side after racing home for a shower and a change of clothes. She'd thrown a microwave dinner into heat beforehand, and once she was clean and dressed, she ate the first real meal she'd had in days. She'd been existing on hospital sandwiches from the cafeteria, but after eating one late yesterday, her stomach had revolted, and whenever she thought about eating another one, her gag reflex had her dry reaching.

As she exited the lifts and walked to the cubicle that she'd left him in, she found the bed empty. She ran to the nurse stationed at the counter. "Where is he? Where's my husband?" she asked unable to stop the panic in her voice.

The woman behind the desk looked up at her with concern, "I'm sorry dear, we tried to call you."

Vanessa's legs gave way, and she had to use the counter to hold herself upright. "I'm sorry, what did you just say?"

Nurse Kimberly repeated herself, "We tried to call you. Your husband went into surgery about," she paused to glance at her watch, "a half an hour ago."

Vanessa ran to the restroom near the waiting area, pushed the door open, and ran for the nearest toilet. Holding her hair in one hand, her stomach twisted, and she lost the only reasonable meal she'd eaten in nearly a week. She flushed the toilet, then slid to the floor and sat beside it still holding her hair. She brought her knees to her chest, hugging them tightly. "But I never got to tell him I love him," she cried.

* * *

Lucifer removed Cosmo's garments,

then carefully cradling her in his arms, walked to the rock pool in the corner of his cave and submerged them both. The water was hot, but not so much so that it would blemish his love's flawless skin, although it turned a soft pink which simply added to her allure. He began to wonder if she still tasted like heaven. His cock twitched at the remembered thought of burying his tongue between her luscious folds. She was the only woman, man or beast he had ever loved or would ever love. He cared for his beloved, washing her skin free of the slick slime that covered her delicate flesh, then returned them both to his bed, where he placed her gently in the middle before climbing in behind her. He curled his much larger body around hers ignoring his need to bury himself inside her. He closed his eyes and slept for the first time in decades.

CHAPTER 14

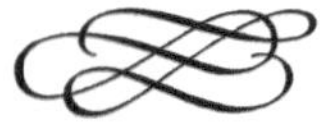

Vanessa paced back and forth though she'd sat for the first few hours. Then as time passed by so slowly, her hopes of seeing Death return to his bed in ICU grew more fragile by the minute. She was well aware that this kind of procedure could take hours, but damn it, she wanted to put an end to this now. She yawned. It had been a really long day, and she was tired of waiting. She reached for the amulet Death had given her to wear. She'd meant to buy some new leather thonging to fix it so she could wear it again. The piece had worn out a couple of months ago, probably closer to a year if she really thought about it. She'd taken to putting it in her pocket and holding it in her palm when she needed reassurance that no matter what, he would be there for her if she needed him. Now, when she yearned to run her fingers over it, she'd left it at home when she'd showered and changed.

* * *

Cosmo stirred as she began to wake up. She immediately recognized the feel of Lucifer curled around her naked body, a solid erection wedged between them. She took a deep breath to strengthen her resolve. 'I will not give in, I cannot give in, I can't give….' Her mantra was interrupted when Lucifer rolled her over and then positioned himself above her. She hated that when it came to him, she could never resist him. As he lowered his head to press his lips to hers, she opened to his tongue's request for access. Suddenly, all the years they'd been apart seemed to melt the walls around Cosmo's frozen heart. A tear slipped from the corner of her eye, fell to the pillow and then the back of Lucifer's hand in the form of tiny diamonds. He broke the kiss, "Shhhh," he pleaded with her, "Don't cry my beloved, you know it breaks me inside to see you cry." He ran his thumb ran under her lashes to wipe away her sadness.

"I can't stay my love, Death needs me. His time draws near."

Lucifer kissed her with an intensity he hoped would convey how much he'd missed her and how much he still loved her. Then, with a reluctant nod, he rolled off her onto his back. By the time his body met the mattress Cosmo was gone, the only reminders that she had been there at all, were three diamond teardrops on the pillow and her discarded clothes on the floor beside the bed. He picked up the gems and placed them on his tongue. He swirled them around inside his mouth tasting their saltiness before tossing them into the rock pool along with the many others he'd thrown there over the centuries.

* * *

Asmodeus had sent a text to his fallen brethren informing them that they needed to have a meeting. He had listened to Ezekiel and Leviathan's plan and was interested to see how things would proceed from there. He led the way to his truck. Climbing in, he entered the address Ezekiel gave him into the GPS and waited for the obnoxious prick to get in and close the door. "So, what exactly are you hoping to find at this woman's place?"

"I don't know yet, but I will when I see it."

Asmodeus drove in silence to the address of the apartment Ezekiel had pulled from the woman's contact details. He was somewhat surprised as to how things appeared to be just falling into the asshole's lap with minimal effort. His phone buzzed to say he'd received a response to his earlier message.

He parked around the corner and pointed to the building they were looking for. He checked the rear-view mirror and exited the vehicle. They turned the corner and crossed the road, keen to get to his rendezvous with his fallen brothers and avoid being caught in the meantime.

As they drew closer to the front door, Asmodeus focused his energy on the lock. His eagerness to see what Ezekiel was seeking was enough to pop the chambers, and the door opened. He extended his finger and pushed as he entered. As Ezekiel tried to cross the threshold, he hit an invisible barrier.

"What the fuck?" he snarled and raised his hands as he tried to put them inside. "Fucking Motherfucker!" he growled, "The bitch has some kind of protection spell in place. It won't let me in. You're going to have to be my eyes."

Asmodeus, still facing the interior smiled at the unforeseen development, and thought to himself, 'Well maybe not everything is going to be as easy as the little fucker thinks.'

He cleared his throat, "Any hints as to what I'm looking for?"

Ezekiel wasn't happy about not having access, but with no alternative, he explained, "If the female were true to her word about being the wife of Death, then she would have to have a key to his realm."

Asmodeus spied the altar in the corner of the room. He had no intentions of touching it at all, and he glanced over his shoulder towards Ezekiel. He was right where he needed to stay for the moment. As he surveyed the rest of the room, he turned in a full circle. Not seeing anything to fit the description of a key, he looked over at the kitchen to see there was nothing on the bench or table. He headed for the bedroom, again studying every object in sight. He opened and closed the bedside table on the side closest to the door, and as he shuffled his foot to make his way around the bed, the soul of his boot tapped on metal as an amulet moved across the carpet hitting the bedpost. He bent over and picked it up, running his thumb over it and feeling its chill. He tucked it into his pocket, and after inspecting a jewelry box on the dresser, he found what he was looking for - a piece of ancient druid history.

As he pulled the door shut behind himself, he passed the piece of gold to Ezekiel, who flipped it over and over in his hand. "I knew it," he jogged back to the truck ahead of Asmodeus.

"Yeah you did, didn't you?" Asmodeus

chuckled as he hit the button to unlock the central locking system.

* * *

Eleven hours, seventeen minutes and twenty-three seconds. Vanessa watched as the second hand ticked by on the clock above the nurse's station. She stood as she watched a doctor wearing scrubs walk towards her, his hair in perfect waves, even after wearing a surgical cap for hours. She was holding her breath as he stopped at the counter. She heard him ask the Matron something and then looked over his shoulder at her, but when his shoulders curved in defeat, she knew the news wasn't going to be good.

"Mrs. McDuffie, I'm one of the doctors that performed surgery on your husband. I'm terribly sorry, he was doing so well until the end. We had some complications, and he didn't make it." The doctor tried to catch Vanessa as she stumbled backward dropping into the seat behind her. "Nurse, I need assistance here."

Vanessa waved them away, "No, No... I'm fine. It's just a shock." She picked up her jacket and helmet from under her chair and headed for the lift.

"Mrs. McDuffie, would you like to say your goodbyes? I can have one of the nurses escort you to see him."

"No thank you, he's not here anymore. He's gone," Vanessa said, her bottom lip trembling. She needed to get out of here now before he came looking for her. She had no idea how long it would be before he found her, but she wasn't in the mood today. Her emotions were too damn raw.

* * *

Cosmo appeared in the operating theatre. The room was empty, except for the nurse in charge of counting and checking all the instruments and her broken son. She moved to the side of the table and lowered the sheet to look at his handsome face. She placed her palm on his cheek, then brushed a stray piece of hair from his temple. She loved all of her children equally, but she had a special place in her heart for her son, the God of Death. She kissed his forehead, held his hand and whispered, "Time to go home, my son. This is the last life you will live that is not your own. You have fulfilled your lessons, and I apologize, for this one was not your lesson to learn, but yours to suffer none the less. You have earned the love and loyalty of your wife through this final sacrifice."

CHAPTER 15

Asmodeus walked calmly into the bar on Main Street. It was dark and damp inside, and he could smell the musty carpet from the previous night's spilled beer. He fucking hated this place, but Belphegor was a glutton as charged and he was weak-willed when it came to vices such as booze, drugs, women and Rock 'n' Roll. He waited for his eyes to grow accustomed to the dim lighting, then looked to the big nasty looking biker behind the bar.

Belphegor put the tea-towel over his shoulder, a glass in the dish rack, then nodded his head towards a table in the back. He put a full bottle of tequila on the bar and a tray of shot glasses next to it. He turned, taking the phone off the hook and walked around to the front door to lock it. With the bottle and glasses, he followed Asmodeus to the back table where the others were waiting.

Asmodeus looked at his fallen brethren, they were all there except for one. He looked at each of them one at a time thankful that his charge had been lust, unlike Abadon who was just outright lazy. He looked as if he hadn't washed his clothes in a week, and as he slouched back in his chair, Asmodeus was pretty sure it was Abadon's body odor offending his nose. He had been rightfully charged. He wore sloth in the same pathetically laid-back way as if he was making a fashion statement.

Next, his eyes fell on Mammon, as he lifted his third shot to his lips, in-between pouring the five other shot glasses, only half full. Asmodeus tilted his to the side to send the message that Mammon's greed had not gone unnoticed. How could anyone miss it when every finger is covered in bling, and you're wearing fur in summer? He shook his head, then met the eyes of Aamon. They were still judgemental and cold as ice, his rage and wrath just under the surface and barely contained.

Belzebub spoke through the silence, "Where's the first, the almighty Lucifer?"

Asmodeus rolled his eyes at the fallen charged with envy, "Well unless I'm mistaken, they still don't have phone reception in hell," he said with a sharp tongue.

* * *

Vanessa pulled her bike up in front of her apartment, switched it off and removed her helmet then just sat there looking around. For some strange reason, everything seemed different. The trees didn't seem so green, the sky didn't look so blue, and her Kawasaki Ninja had lost its appeal. She'd never get to share any of this with Death. It would seem that history would repeat itself over and over, never giving him an opportunity to love the world as she did. She dismounted and walked to her front door with concrete in her boots and led in her heart. She began to strip after closing the front door, tossing each piece of clothing to the floor as it was pulled free.

With her soul weighed down, she turned on the shower and stepped in. She was exhausted. She felt sick and was unbelievably heartbroken. The man in the ICU hospital bed was gentle, he was caring, and he made her smile even when she didn't feel like she had it in her. His touch was soft, and in the past week, she had grown to crave it.

If only they could find some sort of middle ground, a place where she could still live a life with the excitement of discovering new things at the same time spending eternity showing Death how to really live.

The water began to get cold, so she turned the shower off, dried herself then climbed into bed. Maybe if she slept for a while, everything would look better when she woke. If nothing else she might be able to think straight.

* * *

Ezekiel sat in Dominic's car down the street from Vanessa's apartment. He'd been following her waiting for his opportunity. Even though he had the key to Death's realm, he wanted insurance, and Vanessa would give him the leverage he might need if things turned to shit, so he continued to watch and wait for his opportunity to make a move. He lifted the bottle of whiskey to his lips and took another belt before recapping it. Checking around himself, he saw very little movement either inside the woman's apartment or on the street. With nothing better to do than watch, he lowered his zipper and began to stroke himself.

* * *

They'd drawn straws while slamming back tequila, as Asmodeus explained about Ezekiel and Leviathan's plan. How the fool had openly bragged about the lengths, the pair had gone to, to secure the demons safe passage to Middle Earth. After hours of discussions between him and his fallen brethren, the decision was made, using pretzel sticks from behind the bar, to draw straws.

Asmodeus had stepped up to take Abadon's night to watch over the young witch. He didn't trust the lazy prick to stay awake long enough to keep an eye on her, or the weasel sitting in the car down the street. He leaned against the tree in a neighbor's backyard, cutting sections from an apple with a razor-sharp blade with the owner's guard dog at his feet, dreaming about the female Rottweiler from across the road. In all the information he had shared with his fallen brothers, he neglected to mention that he was the one with the key to Death's realm. The reports were that she hadn't ventured outside the walls of her apartment in nearly five days.

* * *

Vanessa looked at her phone again contemplating reaching out to Zandra. Due to her constant moving around, she tried to avoid making friends that she would later have to disconnect with and never see again. Although in the beginning, she had made a solid attempt to ignore the wife of Death's older brother Destiny, the woman was persistent in her pursuit of Vanessa's friendship, even if Zandra only used the excuse of needing to know she was okay, without ever asking for her location. Circumstances had aligned her life with that of

Death's family, and no matter how hard she wanted to disassociate from being involved, it seemed damn near impossible.

After spending a melancholy, however many days it had been, locked in her apartment she needed to go to the store. The freezer was now empty and for how bad she was feeling she knew it was inevitable that her periods would be visiting in the next few days. Her breasts felt swollen and tender.

Vanessa had just climbed out of the shower when she heard her phone beep. She wrapped one towel around her body and another twisted around her hair.

VANESSA,

MEGAN'S NOT GOOD,
 On route to the hospital,
 Will keep you updated.
 Zandra xoxox

. . .

VANESSA READ THE MESSAGE AND QUICKLY responded asking which hospital and explaining that she'd just settled into her new location.

Vanessa heard her phone beep again, this time with the name of the hospital. She was in mixed minds about what to do. She was drawn to the comradery of Megan, Zandra, and JT, but could she risk Death being there? It was a hospital and his family after all. Realizing the chances were high, she played his words over in her mind, "One day I'll make you stop running from me," and her heart sped up at the replayed threat. She just wasn't sure if she was ready to face losing him again. It hurt too much, and after everything that had happened between them, she knew she would never be able to tell him no again. The drive to the hospital was about an hour, and if she was careful, she could hide. She raced to the bedroom of her small apartment, quickly dressed, then pulled a wig down from the top of the cupboard.

Vanessa parked her wheels underground in the hospital's carpark, then removed her gloves and helmet. She pulled at the wig gently to ensure it was securely in place, threw her bag over her shoulder and locked her helmet in the side-saddle.

Standing with her hands on her hips she shook her head thinking 'I must be crazy.' Her gut was telling her this was a bad idea, and her heart was racing as she walked up to the elevator and pushed the button.

* * *

Asmodeus followed two cars behind Ezekiel who was sitting on Vanessa's ass. The idiot was sure to be seen following that closely. He pulled into a carpark on the same level as the woman now removing her helmet. A sudden surge of lust made him hiss. Death's female was all leather covered curves. If he didn't think Death would dismember him and scatter the pieces from the North to the South Pole, then he'd chase some action with her himself. He watched Ezekiel sink down low in the driver's seat of his parked vehicle. Asmodeus knew Vanessa wouldn't recognize him, so he jumped out and quickly ran for the lift.

* * *

Death spun when the air shifted behind him. His mother had given him the time and space to recover from his time spent in Middle Earth. He knew the general area of where Vanessa had relocated to. Although he thought at first, it was purely coincidence that he woke in a hospital bed. After thinking it over, there was no reason for that hospital bed to be in the hospital that Vanessa was at.

"So, what now mother?" he asked, his voice filled with disdain.

"You must go to your brother's side. Destruction needs you. Focus your mind on him and go to him now. You need to let him know that I have sent you to reassure him that the Reaper has no interest in what is his." Cosmo smiled at her second eldest son. "Remember, everything happens for a reason, a season or a lifetime." On her last word, Cosmo disappeared.

"I fucking hate it when you talk in riddles," he said to the already empty space.

He closed his eyes and focused on finding Destruction.

* * *

Zandra gave out a low whistle as she watched the elevator doors open; a sexy blonde with curves swaggered out in black leathers, wearing dark sunglasses. Damn, what she wouldn't give to rock that look. The woman strode straight up to her. Zandra laughed, "Oh My Fucking God! Vanessa?"

Vanessa lifted her sunglasses briefly to show her full face with a smirk. "None other," she replied.

"Love the new look, but do you really think it's enough to keep you safe?" Zandra doubted her friend's confidence in her attempt to remain hidden.

Zandra saw Destiny turn his head in her peripheral vision. Next thing, Iva was passed off to her, and he was on the move. Everything seemed to be moving in slow motion. In the blink of an eye, Death had appeared in the doorway behind Troy, and he looked pissed.

He pushed Destiny out of the way and stormed up to Vanessa. He then placed his arm around her waist and spun her on her heels. She lost her footing and landed in his embrace, with surprise. He captured her lips as she tried to fight him off, then with no regard for the laws they lived by, they vanished.

Zandra jumped up, "Shit! Shit! Do something Des, he took her! She wasn't ready yet. Do something. You have to help her."

Des reached Zandra and held both of his girls to reassure them everything would be alright. "I'm sorry Zan, there's nothing I or anyone else can do for her now. It's between her and Death."

It may have sounded callous, but Troy was glad that his brother was gone and otherwise occupied, even if it was at Vanessa's expense. His Megan would be upset about it when she found out, but they had bigger things to worry about.

* * *

Asmodeus walked out of the lift behind the blonde, watching the way her hips swayed. His lust for her could be measured by the bite marks the teeth of his zipper made. The further she moved away from him the stronger the pull to follow until he saw the man standing ahead of her. 'Fuck!'

he thought as he diverted towards a door marked Emergency Exit only a few feet away. He changed course at the last moment when the door opened, and two more men blocked his escape. He ducked around a corner and, with his back to Death and Destruction, began feeding coins into a snack machine. The look in Death's eyes was murderous as he neared his wife. He saw Death wrap his arm around her waist as his mouth crashed down on hers. His hand fisted in the blonde's hair, and the last thing he witnessed was her long auburn curls fall free as Death dropped the wig to the floor and they disappeared.

CHAPTER 16

Ezekiel jogged out of the carpark and around the front of the building to enter through the front entrance. He'd seen that doublecrossing fallen bastard just as he'd made it into the lift before the doors closed. He'd watched the red digital numbers change as it ascended to the ground floor of the hospital until they came to a stop. He had to presume that they had gotten out as the lift was now returning to the parking garage. "Fucking prick," he mumbled as his head began to throb from all the booze he'd consumed. As he staggered inside almost out of breath, his feet froze to the spot. The sweat from overexertion trickled down his face from his temples. He leaned over with his hands on his knees, trying not to throw up as he watched an agitated Death storm towards Vanessa, mere moments before they both vanished into thin air.

* * *

Death lost control of himself as he recognized Asmodeus from the corner of his eye. He had no idea what the fallen was doing so close to his wife, but something inside of him snapped. Unable to stop himself he strode with purpose, towards the one capturing the attention of his body, heart, and mind. His soul mate would not deny him any longer.

* * *

Vanessa lost her balance as she was spun around to meet the glare of Death's stare. Before she could regain her footing, his lips covered hers as he expressed his frustration, his desire, and his dominance. As she tried to fight it, fight him, fight… it consumed her. She was falling through time, through centuries, through space until she landed on a soft mattress naked, and skin to skin. Her mind raced, her body warmed, and her heart melted. Tears stung her eyes as she cried out, "I come to you," she sobbed, placing her hands on either side of his face. "Of my own free will." She finally surrendered.

Hearing those words come from Vanessa's mouth was like a kick to the chest. His scarred and damaged soul miraculously felt whole for the first time since… ever. It was short lived as his beautiful redhead angel admitted, "I'm scared."

"Shhh baby, I am too." He kissed her from her lips, along her jaw to a spot just under her ear. He whispered, "I've always been scared that you would forever run from me. I've always been scared that I wouldn't find you. But this – you and me, we'll get it right. If you put half the energy into learning to love me as you did running away from me, then I can live with that." he nipped her playfully before kissing a path to her soft pink nipples, to tease them with slow circles and a flick of his tongue.

Vanessa's back arched with the pleasure over the attention her sensitive buds were receiving, making her moan. Death shifted his knee encouraging his wife to spread her thighs. No longer denying Death, she opened herself wide. Her mind, body, heart, and soul were his for the claiming. He relinquished his hold over her plump mounds, working his way back up her body, admiring the flush of pink in her cheeks and the ruby in her kiss-swollen lips. He wondered if he would find colors to match, when later he parted her labia, to taste her desire fully.

"I've been hard for you since I last saw you." he kissed.

"I've missed you," she confessed.

"Are you wet for me?" he asked sliding his hand down between them, his fingers brushing against glistening folds.

Vanessa lowered her eyes, embarrassed at how wet she knew she was.

"Don't," he demanded. "Don't you ever hide from me again."

She met his eyes, then licked her lips preparing to say something... Her mind blanked as Death's shaft nudged at her opening. With a swirl of his hips, Death's solid desire was buried to the hilt inside Vanessa's vessel. Lowering to his elbows he intertwined their fingers, his forehead touched hers, it was like a melding of souls, a joining of hearts and an unspoken acceptance of minds. Unable to stay still any longer, desperate for her lover to move and fix the burning ache of arousal, she clenched her inner muscles. On a growl, Death slid almost free of Vanessa's body. In fear that her lover would leave her in need, she raised her legs and laced them at his back. Her hips rose from the mattress, using her feet for leverage, closing the distance between them. Pushed to the edge of his restraint, Death plunged deep, pumping forcefully. Their combined cries and moans filled the room as he thrust them both over the edge of ecstasy together. Vanessa's walls repeatedly hugged his love for her as he spilled his essence deep, in long hard surges. Spent and fulfilled, he rolled them gently, still encased within his woman's body. For the first time in weeks he could breathe, but at the same time, everything about her took his breath away.

Vanessa tried to stifle a yawn against Death's chest but failed. Placing his lips to her forehead, he whispered, "Sleep Angel, for you will need your strength. I've only just begun to show you how much I love you." Vanessa's eyes fluttered closed in the safety of Death's embrace.

* * *

Ezekiel's temper seethed, bubbling and frothing in his gut. Swiftly he turned on his heel and exited the hospital. Pausing briefly beside the shrubs aligning the footpath, his body expelled the remnants of booze sitting in the pit of his stomach. Wiping his mouth with the back of his hand, he regained his composure and headed for where he'd parked his car.

A short while later he watched Asmodeus step out of the lift. In his hand, Ezekiel brandished the broken bottle that he'd used to rinse his mouth out. Pissed with how things had gone down in the reception area of the hospital, he'd smashed it against the concrete pillar beside his vehicle. When he looked at the jagged edges, he wondered how long it took a fallen angel to heal. "Fucking Cocksucker you can swallow my hardened dick!" he slurred, slicing his weapon through the air making contact with Asmodeus on three out of four attempts to harm him. Asmodeus fell to the ground, with glass protruding from his side.

Ezekiel rummaged through the injured man's pockets looking for his keys. If he were without transport, then he would be left no other options than to stay put or wait for one of his brothers to come to his aid. Ezekiel pulled a handful of metal from Asmodeus's jeans, he gave them a quick glance as he prepared to toss them as far away as his arm would reach. As his arm pulled back the emblem heated in his palm, and he frowned when it continued to grow warmer to his touch.

"You double-crossing motherfucker," he screamed, raising his boot, and bringing it down to connect with Asmodeus's face. "Lights out asshole." Sinking his hand into his pocket, he retrieved the worthless gold piece Asmodeus had misled him to believe was the key to Death's realm, tossing it onto the chest of the now unconscious fallen.

* * *

Death stirred, reaching out to his wife in his semi-hard state, to find the space beside him empty. Panic threatened to close his throat, as he flashed out of bed to the bathroom, then the kitchen. There in front of an open fridge door, stood Vanessa in nothing but a towel, searching the shelves for something to eat.

"Well I guess it looks like fruit salad," she mumbled to herself as she collected pieces of fruit from a bowl beside a dozen cans of energy drinks. Placing her selection on the bench next to the fridge, she began to search the drawers for a knife and the cupboards for a cutting board and dish. Death watched in awe as his female began to hum to herself while dissecting the fruit into sections. Watching the sway of her towel-covered curves shimmying as she sliced and diced fruit, made him hotter than brimstone in hell. One minute, he was on the other side of the kitchen, the next he was behind her, his impressive cock settled into the crease of her rounded cheeks. Growling in her ear as his arms circled her waist, they then rose to cup her luscious breasts. Vanessa swatted at his hands playfully, "I'm starving, how about you?" she popped a piece of peach into her mouth, moaning at how sweet and juicy it was.

Death tilted her head so he could lick the spilled drops from the corner of her mouth, lifting her into his arms as she protested. "Hey!" she objected swallowing the mouthful she had.

"I'm famished," Death admitted. He laid Vanessa on the kitchens table, then he returned carrying the fruit salad. Lifting a section of pear to his lips, he bent down to share it with Vanessa, biting the piece in half as her lips met his. "Mmmm, that's good," he confessed watching her eat her portion before finding a piece of peach. Using his free hand, he opened the front of the towel exposing Vanessa's pebbled gems, and his eyes met hers. Distracted by how handsome he was, she gasped as the cold flesh was painted onto her nipples. Death's head descended to trail his artistic strokes with his tongue. He pulled out the chair at the head of the table, slid Vanessa's ass to the edge, and he positioned her feet on his spread thighs, opening her wide. Collecting another piece of peach, he watched Vanessa jump as he made contact with her splayed labia. Lowering his lips, he groaned at the succulent taste of peaches mixed with her natural nectar. Death devoured her, making her scream as he fucked her with his tongue, then scalloped it to torture her swollen exposed clit. His thumbs opened her further, and he sat back briefly to admire his female's secret place. He smiled at her beautiful pink orchid.

Aching so badly he could no longer ignore his own need, he stood, kicking the chair away. Lifting Vanessa's legs over his forearms, he buried himself fully in one fluid drive of his hips. Vanessa cried out, "Reaper!" It was a name that on anyone else's lips would have ignited his anger, on Vanessa's tongue, however, it sounded seductive and sensual, adding an extra edge to his hunger to satisfy and to be satisfied. Vanessa's head tilted, her back curved and she let out a scream, as her pussy convulsed around him. Her juices coated his shaft and intensified the slapping sounds of Death's pounding thrusts. One, two, three more and he arched his back howling at the ceiling as he fell over the edge. Covering Vanessa's shaking body, he rolled his pelvis against her throbbing clit. Sobbing, she wrapped her arms around her husband as his head rested in the center of her chest.

"Fuck me, at this rate you'll be the death of me woman," he chuckled.

Pushing up off Vanessa, Death collected the chair then lifted her into his lap. Placing the untouched fruit in front of them, he began to feed her as she relaxed into his hold.

"I think the only thing I will miss will be my Ninja," she sighed, with resignation.

"What's a Ninja?" he sputtered, hoping he wouldn't have to kill it.

"It's my sexy ride, I only just purchased it," she told him.

Incapable of resisting the saddened expression on her face, he offered, "We can bring it here."

She laughed, looking around, "Yeah right, and where exactly am I going to ride it?"

Death had already been thinking about the possibilities, and he saw no reason why they couldn't live happily in the same manner his brothers had been given. However, he would need to confer with his mother before he said anything to Vanessa. Not about to give her any false hopes, he would take care of that as soon as he had the chance.

"Well, for now, why don't we bring it here? At least it will be safe until we make any decisions." He squeezed her thigh and lifted her off his lap. Death's fingers were drawn to her red curls, his head dipping to place a kiss on her soft lips. As he broke the kiss and opened his eyes, he gave her a devilish smile, "Fuck, dressed like that I'm already hard. Come on before we end up naked again."

Vanessa looked down at herself to find she was dressed in the leather she'd worn to hospital, boots and all. "Neat trick," she smiled.

"Hold onto me and don't let go. I need you to picture your apartment." His thumb brushed her jawline, "Okay?"

Vanessa put her arms around Death and cupped his ass cheeks then nodded, "Got it." She only swayed slightly as everything turned black and then suddenly she was standing in her new bedroom.

"Sorry, best I could do," she shrugged.

* * *

Aamon pulled the glass free from Asmodeus's side, removing his own shirt, he scrunched it up and pushed it against the wound. "Are you ready to give up the secret you've been keeping from us?" he asked, applying pressure. "Hold this," he said, helping his injured brother to his feet, and walking him over to his double-parked SUV. Aamon opened the rear door and ushered Asmodeus inside, "Get in."

Asmodeus did as he was told, only because he knew the fallen brother getting in behind the steering wheel was not the sort to mess with.

"You going to tell me who did this and why?" he barked over his shoulder as he put it into gear and released the handbrake.

"Put me back together, and I'll explain while you're playing doctors and nurses," Asmodeus wheezed as the vehicle rode over a speed bump at the exit to the parking garage.

Asmodeus must have passed out briefly because the next thing he knew, Aamon was dragging him out of the back seat bitching under his breath, "Fuck me, you can pay to have that shit cleaned."

With his arm around Aamon's shoulder, he staggered through the back door of Belphegor's bar. Falling onto the sofa that sat in the office out back, he stretched out to the full length, his boots overhanging the arm. Belphegor entered behind them and cursed under his breath while opening the safe. Lifting out a small pot of red powder he griped, "Don't waste it."

Aamon snarled at Belphegor, "I'll use what I need to fix him. He'd do the same for any of us, and you know it."

Grabbing the neck of Asmodeus's shirt

he tore it down the middle, swearing, "Fuck man, this is going to sting like a bitch!" He took a pinch of powder from the jar, then sprinkled it over the wound. On contact, the powder began to froth, sizzle and burn. "FU…CK!" Asmodeus shouted. "Okay, get it off, I'm good, I'm good." Belphegor nodded at Aamon, confirming that the powder had done its job.

Panting heavily, Asmodeus, pushed himself up into a sitting position, tore the rest of his shirt off and used it to wipe his side. "Thanks," he stuck his hand out, and Aamon grabbed it, helping him to stand.

With a brotherly clap on the back, Aamon sidestepped him to pass the container back to Belphegor.

"Blood of my blood, I am indebted to you both." Asmodeus lowered his eyes to the floor knowing he had lied by omission to his fallen brethren.

Aamon stood tall in front of him and demanded, "Blood of my blood, I call you on your debt to me."

Asmodeus's eyes lifted to those of Belphegor then swung to back to Aamon. "I don't accept your bargain. I, unfortunately, owe you all an explanation. How long before the others can get here?"

"They never fucking left," Belphegor complained.

CHAPTER 17

Ezekiel sat outside Vanessa's apartment with the key swinging from his fingers in a hypnotic sway. Staring deep in thought, he was taken by surprise when the front door opened, and Vanessa stood on the threshold, glancing around as though looking for something. He quietly slid from the front seat and clipped the door on the first latch to avoid making any sound. When she turned and walked to the mailbox at the side of the premises, she left the door open. The only trouble was, he couldn't enter because of the witch's spells. Unsheathing a dagger he'd bought with a specific purpose in mind, he waited for her to return to the front door so he could jump her. Everything seemed to happen so fast. The moment her back was to him, he sprang forth from around the opposing corner of the apartment building. He wrapped his arm around her waist and with the dagger at her throat he snarled, "Don't try anything funny. Bring down your barriers witch," he demanded, not wanting to be seen on the street doing what had to be done.

Vanessa gasped at the feel of the blade at her throat, and she reversed the chant she had used to protect her place from those whom would seek to do her harm. Ezekiel reached out his elbow not willing to simply believe her. It passed through the doorway without hindrance. Dragging Vanessa along with him he entered her apartment, kicking the door shut once inside.

The minute the front door slammed, Ezekiel shifted the blade. Still using a vice-like grip on Vanessa, he slid it along his jugular and then plunged it into his own heart. He took Vanessa to the floor with Dominic's lifeless body. He began to chant in his mind, creating a black hole in the carpet and Vanessa and Ezekiel fell through, leaving only the corpse of the dead man behind.

* * *

Death had successfully delivered Vanessa's motorcycle to Destiny's garage which was as good a place as any to store it temporarily. Returning to Vanessa's apartment as quick as he could shadow shift, he materialized in her bedroom and found open bags packed with clothes. Everything looked to be ready to go, so he walked out of the room heading for the rest of the apartment. Death's heart sped up on discovering the man in the entryway to the lounge room. "Who the fuck are you, and where the fuck is my wife?" he asked through clenched teeth.

Rolling the body over, he studied the dagger buried in the man's chest. It looked like some sort of ritualistic weapon. Knowing his wife's history of the Arts, he panicked. There was no sign of her anywhere. Fearing for her whereabouts in relation to the deceased, he searched for her altar. If she had run of her own free will, she would never leave her altar or Grimoire behind. Death found both untouched, "Fuck!"

Death kneeled next to the body then quickly absorbed the soul, taking it to the treasury of souls for release. Confused, he went back to Vanessa's trying to figure out what the fuck was going on. After the time they'd spent together, he didn't want to think that she'd left him again. Had he put too much faith in believing what he wanted to believe, so much so that he'd effectively given her the chance to run yet again?

* * *

Ezekiel knocked Vanessa unconscious when he fell back to hell taking her with him. He landed hard on the dirt floor in the pit of darkness. With no way to see inside the chamber, he closed his eyes, seeking out his hidden body. As though attached by an overstretched bungee cord it pulled him through the rock walls. Similar to an electrical charge his essence slammed back inside his body with a jolt. Gasping, he tried to sit up, though unfortunately, he was too exhausted from his body snatching ordeal to even move his little toe. He blinked three times before his eyelids became too heavy to open, and he succumbed to the uncomfortable fact that he had a rock pressing against the middle of his spine. His last thought was 'Home sweet fucking home. I never missed you one shitty bit.'

* * *

Vanessa slowly stirred. Her head hurt, and her ankle felt as though she'd twisted it. Opening her eyes she attempted to sit up, her head swam, and she thought for a moment she was going to be sick. She must have hit her head when she fell. Her heart rate spiked when it registered in her mind that she was surrounded by pitch black nothingness. What made it worse, was that it was so eerily quiet she could hear her own blood rushing in her ears, only accentuating the pounding in her skull. Pushing herself to her feet, she dusted off the sand like substance from the floor. Holding her hands out in front of herself, she took a tentative step forward then moved her hands outwards as though playing blind man's bluff. Another step and she repeated the process, over and over until finally, her hands met with a wall of rock. Slipping one shoe off, she turned to the right and began to circle her way along the wall hoping to find an exit, all the while praying for Death to come and find her.

Eventually, she kicked something on the floor. She'd completed a full circle of the room. Sinking down to where the sand at her feet met the rock wall, she slipped her discarded shoe back on after brushing the sand off her foot. Tilting her head back she closed her eyes, attempting to convince herself that this was simply a bad dream brought forth by a bump on her head. She was most likely in a hospital bed somewhere with a concussion.

She hoped that no matter where she was, Death would know where to find her.

* * *

Death couldn't sense Vanessa's essence anywhere. It was as though somehow she'd managed to reinstate the wards and barriers that had kept him from her for centuries, he thought it was odd that she didn't take the objects from her altar or her spell book. If she was cloaked from him though, she could be standing in the same room as him, without him even knowing it. Turning a three-sixty he roared, releasing his anger. The walls in the apartment began to split like someone had painted crazy crackle nail enamel on them. There was no doubt Death was so furious he could level the building, but he knew that it would be pointless. As an alternative, he eyeballed the most precious belonging in a witch's possession. Muttering under his breath in case she was somewhere close watching he snarled, "You will come back to me if you ever want your sacred shit returned."

Death strode into the kitchen and opened a drawer; there was nothing of use in the first or second one. However, the third one was golden. Picking up a pair of tongs and a spatula, he continued his rant, pointing at Vanessa's Grimoire, "You are coming with me, whether you like it or not. So unless you want to wind up in my fireplace, you will come along peacefully."

He lifted the four corners of the altar cloth and placed it on the floor, the bowl of salt spilled throughout the herbs. The crescent-shaped boline, a sickle-shaped, curved-bladed knife with a white handle, had cut into the fabric and her wand's clear quartz crystal was glowing red and facing on an angle that pointed towards the shell of the dead man. On bended knee, Death used the acquired utensils to add Vanessa's Grimoire to the contents of the cloth. Mission accomplished, he tied the corners into a knot then disappeared back to his own world. The human realm no longer held any appeal for him. He would not tolerate the trickery of humans, especially of the female kind. His heart no longer cared what happened on Middle Earth. Determined to show Vanessa the extent of his powers, he planned to wait in his realm until she returned to him.

CHAPTER 18

Death opened the vault, swinging it open just enough to drop Vanessa's belongings inside the Treasury of Souls, before slamming it shut again. Until she returned to retrieve them, they would be the last things he collected.

Throwing his duties in a pile by the fireplace, the pages flipped open as though taunting him. He turned his back on them, he'd deal with them later. Vanessa's betrayal made his gut burn, and his skin seemed to be overly tight.

He flipped off the list of names he was due to collect. The sliding door on his heart had opened wide, it had let Vanessa walk-through, and in his own stupidity, he'd welcomed her with open arms. Sadly, he hadn't seen the set of steak knives she was hiding with her leather curves and her seductive smile. "Fucking witch," he growled, knowing how much he wanted to replace his love for her with hate but couldn't.

In Death's absence, the world began to slip into unknown territory. While people continued to die their essences continued to clutter up the human realm.

* * *

Barry Collins had spent most of his adult life hiding from the police. His psychotic breaks had left him with black spots in his memory, always waking up to find himself in yet another situation. His grandmother had always told him it was because of his fucked up DNA coding. As the daughter of a minister, his grandfather had forbidden her to have an abortion after being gang-raped at the precious age of nineteen. His grandfather's belief was that the good Lord made everything happen for a reason and that the unborn fetus could turn out to be the next president or the person who discovers a cure for cancer. Oh, how wrong that sanctimonious prick had been! Barry had been nothing but trouble from the first breath of oxygen he had stolen. He'd been the cause of his mother's death, for which his grandmother had blamed him on every anniversary of the day she'd died, "Yeah, happy birthday to me hey grandma you old bitch." He continued to scrub his hands, today was his forty-third birthday. Celebrations had obviously been in full swing most of the night. He glanced at the body of the naked female on his bed.

So that he never forgot his party for two, he dried his hands and etched another notch into the timber frame of the bed.

He was tired, and his head hurt, maybe if he just laid down for a moment, everything would just stop. He beat his skull several times with the fist that was wrapped around the blade. He wished, after twenty-two years of this shit that someone would find him and stop him from playing these games.

The door exploded, and a woman with a dark blue vest entered the room, "Don't move asshole!"

Barry lifted his head to the ceiling and began to cry, "Thank you, Jesus. Thank you, Jesus."

"Drop the knife and get down on your hands and knees now motherfucker!" A guy wearing a matching vest entered the room.

Barry's head buzzed with anger at having another man in his domain. As he attempted to lunge at him, the female opened fire. To his relief, all he could think as his body exploded with fire was, "Dear Lord forgive me. I'm coming home broken so you can fix me." His last breath seeped out of his body as his blood pooled on the floor.

Four hours later, Barry was transferred to a cold slab in the mortuary. As the young assistant, Shane prepared his body for an autopsy, he leaned over and opened Barry's mouth. He checked his teeth for dentures and then prepared a dental impression plate. Sitting the plate aside on a tray, he turned back to the corpse, but before he could close Barry's mouth he began to cough, and a fine mist escaped as Shane inhaled.

Shane whipped of his surgical glove and dug in his pocket for his inhaler. Administering two puffs, he stood up straight and frowned. Shane's eyes returned to the man on the table. He walked to the clipboard on the tray, lifted it and started to read, justifiable shooting by Detective Jennifer Lowan. He put the chart back down and as he walked towards the door, he began removing the blue apron.

* * *

Sonja was floating, though she didn't care, because the pain had stopped. Noise from below drew her attention; the loud sounds of gunfire hurt her ears. Terrified, she curled up into a ball and sank down into the crawl space under the bed. She screamed as feet moved too close to her hiding space. She didn't understand what was happening. The last thing she remembered was having a drink with a man in a bar. She couldn't even recall his name. A knife was kicked, sliding it under the edge of the bed, making her stare in horror as it passed through her arm to spin on the tiles. Rolling to avoid the blade and being discovered, it became abundantly clear that she could no longer feel the coolness resonating from the floor. Fear struck at the sinking sensation that something was wrong, very wrong. She lifted her hand up to her mouth, parted her lips and bit down on the back of her knuckles hard. Nothing. Not a damn thing, no pain, no feeling. Scampering out from her hiding place, she rose beside the bed, and on seeing her own body bloodied and dead, she doubled over screaming. The people moving around in the room either chose to ignore her or simply didn't see her. She tried to touch them, and her hand passed through them, causing barely a shudder.

Detective Jennifer Lowan felt a cold chill run over the back of her neck and goose bumps appeared on her skull. She hoped she wasn't getting a summer cold because it sure as shit wasn't the weather. "Over here, I got something!" called the forensic pathologist. "The crease in this mat indicates frequent folding back on itself. He looks to have kept trophies of his victims in a heart-shaped box. There must be at least two or three dozen of them."

Detective Lowan flicked through the photos looking for her sister. Nobody knew the main cause of her investigation was linked to the disappearance of her older sister. It had been the driving force behind her joining the academy in the first place. Hell-bent on solving the cold case, she'd forgone many relationships to focus on her career and lost countless hours of sleep, all of it corralling to this moment in time. With a sigh and tear-filled eyes, she looked at the ceiling in silent prayer to her long-dead parents. 'I did it, I found her,' she told them. Needing to find air in the closed room, she handed the find back to Derek to bag and tag them. Her justifiable shooting no longer an issue for her to have to live with, she'd simply eliminated yet another one of society's parasites.

Sonja watched as the female-headed for the door, and not wanting to go anywhere near the male components inside the room, she ran towards her dodging the opposite species. One of the men stood and took an unexpected step sideways. As she tried to avoid him, her body fell into that of Detective Jennifer Lowan.

* * *

Using Shane's connection to the police department, he acquired the address and details of one Detective Jennifer Lowan. His nerves were frayed as the original owner of the body kept fighting him. The constant prayers rattling around in his brain were making him insane. He just couldn't figure out how to shut the fucker up, other than to slice the shithead's throat. While ever he needed this body to move around that was never going to happen. Asshole bible bashers, 'do they not know God fucks the Queen's corgi's?'

He opened the fridge and pulled out a small packet of ham and a beer. Cracking the top of the Corona, he slugged back half of it before opening the ham and scoffing it down. Tossing the empty plastic onto the pristine sink, he held a conversation in his head with his cohabiter, 'Yeah well that's just too damn bad, I do eat meat and drink beer, so suck it up ya pussy.' Finishing the remainder, he washed down the salty taste of the cold cuts.

* * *

Detective Jennifer Lowan's hand shook as she pushed the key in to unlock her door. Her nerves were shot to hell after seeing the picture of her sister, beaten and mutilated by a monster. Although the bastard was dead, her stomach still rolled, and her heart ached for what Laney must have gone through before she died.

Opening the door to her apartment, she stepped inside and bolted it, engaging the safety locks and chains. One could never be too careful in her business. You never knew when one of the germs she'd put away would get out on parole and come looking for vengeance.

Switching on the light, she kicked off her boots at the front door. Walking to the fridge, she grabbed a bottle of beer and used the corner of the bench to knock the top off. Lifting it to her lips, she glanced from the corner of her eye to see the already empty bottle and the packet of meat. Sitting her Corona on the bench, she turned, reaching for her gun.

"Ahh-Ahh-Ah Detective!" Barry said, before subduing her with a taser he had located in her bedside drawer.

The shock to Jennifer's system dislodged Sonja, and Barry's eyes squinted in her direction. "Happy Birthday to me, happy birthday to me. Whore, whore, WHORE!" he yelled moving towards Sonja's presence. His hand tried to enclose around Sonja's neck, but it passed straight through.

"Never mind bitch. You watch what I to do to the good detective here, and I'll sleep better knowing you'll never rest in peace, slut."

* * *

Cosmo appeared in Jennifer's kitchen, "Yeah, happy birthday cocksucker," she said placing both hands either side of Shane's face. Leaning in quickly she inhaled, pulling the foreign soul free from the hijacked body. Cosmo froze time to allow her to deliver the malicious murderer to his keeper.

Again falling at the feet of Lucifer's

throne, Cosmo coughed and regurgitated the diseased soul into Lucifer's realm. She shivered, then vanished to fix the rest of the problems created by her son's insubordination.

On returning to the place where time stood still, she whispered into the ears of both the female and the male. "He is the key to your happiness, you will never be alone again," she told Jennifer.

"She is the key to your future, take good care of her," she explained to Shane. Then as she waved the spirit of Sonja into her embrace, she told them both, "You know not how you came to be here, only that you need to be. Take things slow and let love grow." Cosmo collected the fallen tear and placed it into Shane's palm. With Cosmo's blessing, "Use this when the time is right." With that request, Cosmo disappeared with Sonja.

Jennifer and Shane blinked several times glancing around the place, confused as to why they were there. Shane offered, "I'm starving, would you join me for dinner?"

Jennifer feeling normal for the first time

since her sister's death replied, "I'd love to. Can you give me five minutes to change?"

Shane smiled, "Sure." When Jennifer walked away, Shane's fist pumped the air with excitement. Something sharp dug in between his fingers. Opening his clenched fist, he found a perfectly formed diamond. Feeling his back pocket, he pulled out his wallet and deposited it into the corner of the zip section.

* * *

Cosmo found Death slouched at his dining table, his hand resting palm flat on the surface. 'How could she fake something so real?' he asked himself again.

"Do you realize the damage you are doing wallowing in your self-pity? Do you love her enough to go and find her?" she asked.

"You know very well I've loved her for more than one lifetime. But..." his words trailed off, not really wanting to have this conversation with his mother.

"What if I told you that your females' life and the life of your unborn son depends on you finding her? She needs you now more than ever. I will grant you the same thing I have given to your brothers. The time it will take in Middle Earth to find Vanessa."

"What good will that do? I can't sense her… Anywhere. She's hidden herself from me again."

"No son, this time she did not use her craft."

"How do you know?" he questioned.

"Because I am her goddess, the one she honors when weaving her spells. I am the one who gives them power."

"Get Out!" Death demanded.

"You can sit around here and lose the love of your wife and child while hating me, or you can take what I offer and bring my daughter-in-law and grand-baby home to me. You have three days. Don't waste them."

"I said get out," he seethed.

"If you decide to go, look for the fallen ones, they will guide you," Cosmo said on a sob before fading away.

CHAPTER 19

Vanessa must have fallen asleep, but as she opened her eyes in the dark cavernous space, she knew she wasn't alone. "Who's there?"

Leviathan shifted, "Nobody you would know." Sitting cross-legged only a foot away, he straightened his spine to its full length and rotated his head on his shoulders, cracking his neck. "I will ask the questions, and you will answer them."

"What makes you think I know anything? And just exactly where the fuck am I?" she retorted.

"As Reaper's mistress, you are the key to my reign. I will rid hell of Lucifer, and I shall become the Lord and Master of fire and brimstone. You will never see your husband ever again unless I say so."

"What makes you think holding me prisoner will get you what you want?" Vanessa asked, trying to hide the tremor of fear in her voice.

"I am the chosen demon that sits at the right hand of Lucifer. He trusts me after many years of faithful service. I grow tired of playing with the sinners. I want more." He reached out his hand and ran a finger down Vanessa's arm. She screamed as her skin split open as though he'd cut her with a razor. Leviathan lifted his fingers to his lips and painted them with her blood before licking them clean. "Mmmmm. Your unborn child sweetens your essence. I will bring you food so that your belly may grow round and full."

Vanessa ran her hand along her arm when she felt the blood drip from her fingers, but they came away dry. There was no wound. It had to be mind manipulation, "Fuck you asshole. I won't give you a damn thing, and I'd rather starve to death than give you what you seek."

Leviathan's blow was swift leaving Vanessa unconscious.

* * *

Asmodeus pushed his stiff cock inside the beauty he'd chosen to relieve his tension with for the evening. With her hands against the stall door, he pumped into her with the force of a beast untamed. Raising her onto her tiptoes with every thrust, he clamped his hands on her hips to change the angle. He'd picked the female for her curves and studied the way her ass jiggled with every stroke. Getting closer to the edge he lowered his right hand down between the banshee's thighs to circle her clit. Luckily the noise coming from the rest of the bar was enough to cover her sounds. He heard the band grow louder briefly as someone entered the ladies toilets. Continuing with his quest for the satisfaction he ignored the intruder. Focusing back on the wet pussy as it started to milk his cock. He moaned but was drowned out by her squawking as her first orgasm coincided with a second and more intense one. Three more pumps and he spilled his load inside the condom. After sliding free of her snatch, he slapped her butt cheek as thanks for the ride, then removed the condom, tied it in a knot and deposited it into the sanitary bin behind them. Easing himself back into his jeans and zipping up his fly, he flipped the lock pushing her out of the cubicle. Clearing the stalls, Asmodeus paused on his way to wash his hands.

"Something I can help you with soul eater?" he asked as he resumed his intentions to rid himself of his lustful evidence.

The young lady battered her lashes at Asmodeus in hopes of getting a second round in later, then stormed out the door when Asmodeus chose to ignore her.

Moving at the speed of light, one minute Death was leaning against the wall by the hand dryers, the next he was pushing Asmodeus up against the spot he'd stood in seconds prior. One hand around Asmodeus's throat, the other pulled back ready to punch. "Where is she?"

"Okay, I'm going to plead blonde on this

one Reaper. Where's who? The redhead you stole from the human hospital?"

Deaths grip tightened, "Where's my wife?"

"Alright, alright. Let me go, and we'll tell you what we know."

Asmodeus's heel slid on the tiled floor as Death released his hold on the fallen.

* * *

Ezekiel woke from his comatose state, feeling refreshed, hungry and horny, thinking for a moment of his options. Option A – Satisfy himself. 'Not fucking likely,' he thought. Option B – Locate one of the hounds. 'Again not fucking likely. Those slags bite and tear strips of flesh off as fucking foreplay.' Option C – The pretty redhead. He smiled to himself, "C it is then." He sat up making the rocks fall to the ground around him, and dusting himself off, he made his way to where he knew the female was being held captive.

On entering the chamber, he witnessed the interaction between Leviathan and the witch. Leaving him with more questions than answers, Leviathan was doing a whole heap of 'I'ing, and Ezekiel, who was supposed to be his equal partner, knew there was no 'I' in team. The bastard had lied, only giving some portions of the plan to get him to do the dirty work, while Leviathan would keep the glory.

Betrayed, he got very little satisfaction from watching Leviathan torment the innocent. 'Fucking double-crossing motherfucker. Fuck you.' After Leviathan knocked the witch out, Ezekiel disappeared to appease his next desire… Food!

Slicing another piece of meat from the prisoner, he lifted it to his mouth on the blade. That turned out to be the biggest mistake of his existence. Ezekiel didn't hear Leviathan step up from behind until the larger than normal bluish white skinned hand closed around his. Claiming control of his movement, Leviathan cut off his tongue rendering him speechless.

Leviathan had brought one of the hounds with him, and tossed the amputated muscle towards Deidre, "Here, get rid of this."

Catching it mid-air, Deidre disposed of

it in three bites. Licking her fingers, she moved closer, and with a snarl, she asked, "What about the rest of him?" looking him up and down then focusing her attention on his shriveled dick.

Leviathan tsked, "All in good time Deidre."

* * *

Asmodeus huddled the rest of the fallen into the small office in the back of the bar. Belphegor was the last through the door, bitching and whining about being pulled away from drinking tequila shots from the belly button of a half-naked woman that was laid out like the last supper on top of the bar.

When his eyes landed on Death, he abruptly shut the fuck up, bowing his head in a sign of respect. "Reaper," he acknowledged, kicking Abadon's foot to wake the lazy son of a bitch up.

Wrath cracked his knuckles to indicate he was ready to rumble if that was about to play out. Six fallen sinners and the soul eater all in one small room was an unholy amount of testosterone.

"Here's the deal. I heard a whisper that you guys know where my elusive wife may be hiding out." Death eyeballed each of them, "All except for you Abadon. You're too lazy to lift your own leg to fart, so I doubt you have a fully functional brain. It's probably just as slovenly as the rest of you."

Abadon would have flipped him off, but he couldn't be bothered and simply replied with a shrug, then closed his eyes and dozed off again.

"What's in it for us if we help you?" Mammon, the fallen charged with greed, asked.

"I'll teach you how not to dress like a two-bit pimp," Death responded.

"I'd settle for a day where I don't have some dumb fuck try to pick a fight with me." Aamon, (Wrath) interjected.

"I'd be happy with not seeing your ugly asses in my bar for at least ten years. You pretty boys are messing with my mojo," Belphegor (Gluttony) confessed objectively.

Before anyone else could throw their two cents into the fray, Death put two fingers to his lips and whistled, "Pull your fucking heads in, all of you. You wonder why God banished you from his realm. It's because you squabble like a pack of tuck-shop ladies." [Women who run the school canteen]

Belzebub (Envy) interrupted his statement, setting the record straight. "We were kicked out because we wouldn't satisfy the Almighty's desires."

"That's not my issue, and that's not why I'm here," he glanced around, then added, "I see Lucifer is missing, so I take it he still wants nothing to do with your sorry asses." Folding his arms across his chest, he made his point. "God refuses to lay eyes on you, so that leaves Cosmo and her permission for you to live in Middle Earth. I'm sure my family can make each of your eternities a living hell, so that being said, what do you know?"

CHAPTER 20

Vanessa woke in a furious state of shock. How dare they take her from the man she loved? She began to feel remorse for all the times that she'd evaded him. Tears of anger filled her eyes, but she refused to let them fall. Placing both hands on her belly, she sent up a plea in the hope that Death would not forsake her. He'd told her many centuries ago that he would always come to her. This time, she was praying that he would save them both. Protective instincts over her unborn child began to bubble and brew. If he didn't come for her soon, she would do whatever it took to bust out of wherever the hell they were holding her.

* * *

Cosmo appeared at the pearly gates, "I need to see Him. Inform Him I will be in receiving. Oh and tell him I'm in a hurry."

Peter nodded and vanished as did Cosmo. Within seconds of her feet landing on the floor, the door to her right opened, and the epitome of every woman's wet dream stood on the threshold, with his hands on his hips. Cosmo rolled her eyes, "Always the drama queen G," shaking her head.

"What do you want Cosmo? I thought we had an agreement. You stick to Middle Earth, and I stay out of your way. End of story," he said, looking her up and down with contempt.

"My second eldest son needs your help. His soulmate has gone missing, and it would seem there is trouble brewing on the dawn."

"You seem to be under the misconception that I care about what happens in

Middle Earth, or hell for that matter," he yawned for emphasis.

"Well, you should, if you want these fools to continue to worship your sad sanctimonious ass."

"Why don't you tell me how you really feel?" he said dryly, stepping back out of the way so she could enter his office.

* * *

Asmodeus explained about Ezekiel's escape from Hell, and how he was bent on discovering a way to obtain the key to Death's realm. How they'd seen Death capture the redhead in the hospital… Ezekiel's attack on Asmodeus… the theft of the key.

"What did the host's body look like?" Death was beginning to fear that Ezekiel was responsible for the corpse in Vanessa's lounge room.

Asmodeus confirmed his suspicions by describing the dead man to him. Death knew the only way for a demon to return to Hell was through the host dying. Therefore, he'd caused the male to commit suicide. The only conclusion was, that when the rogue demon had fallen back to where he'd come from, he'd managed to take Vanessa with him. What puzzled him was why?

* * *

Cosmo left her meeting with God with a pounding headache. The man had always affected her that way. Unfortunately, the emotions of love and hate were too closely related that she simply had to concede, he was one man or one God she loved to hate.

Entering Lucifer's throne room, her heart raced, and she blushed at the sinful ideas that popped into her head. Even after an eternity apart she could not deny she loved him. Where God was all pure and sterile, Lucifer was all fire and passion. To her, it was similar to what all women would see as the good-looking football jock versus the bad boy. Holding her breath, she watched as his eyes lifted from the slate floor to meet hers. The desire in his look made her exhale hard as she felt her juices liquefy between her thighs. Damn him, he'd always been able to do that to her. When she glanced at her feet and blinked, he was no longer on his throne. She gasped as his hands circled her waist and spun her to crush her breasts against his chest. His lips covered hers, his tongue running the seam where their mouths met. He wasn't asking for entry, he was demanding it. Her hands landed on his bare chest, this wasn't what she came here for, but it all felt too good to try to resist his touch. 'What had she come for? Why had she stayed away from him for so long?' The thoughts in her head became confused, and the reasons for being in Hell were easily forgotten, the moment his tongue brushed against hers. She moaned and slid her hands up from his chest around his neck pulling him closer.

Death materialized in Lucifer's throne room, shocked at what he'd intruded on. He finally loosened his rage. "What The Fuck are you doing?" he yelled at his Mother.

Cosmo pushed herself free of Lucifer's hold, "I... Um... I" she stammered, at a loss for an explanation.

Death lunged for Lucifer, "You fucking bastard!" With fists clenched, Death intended on playing for keeps. The shrill scream of Cosmo made him pause before he could connect his first hit.

"STOP!" Cosmo fell to her knees sobbing, "He's your father."

"You're not worth my energy," Death pronounced, taking a step back from Lucifer, not understanding why the fallen hadn't moved to retaliate.

"Why didn't you ever tell me Cosmo?" Lucifer asked, wearing a hurt expression.

Death looked from Cosmo to Lucifer, waiting for one of them to explain what it all meant.

Cosmo shook her head as diamonds scattered across the slate. Lucifer and Death took a step towards Cosmo at the same instant, their eyes watching each other warily.

"Don't," Death said in a foreboding tone.

"Son, I would never hurt your mother. I have been in love with her since the beginning of time. She is my Eve as I am her Adam. We once lived together in the heavens with God, but," he paused to help Cosmo stand, "we loved each other more than we loved God."

Cosmo placed her hand on Lucifer's cheek, "I came here to tell you that our grandson is in danger."

Death took a step back from them, shaking his head. The impact of his mother's words sank into his soul. He was the son of the first fallen, the one charged with pride, the Lord of Darkness. Well didn't that just explain everything, except the one thing that bothered him most - the reason his mother had never told him?

There would be plenty of time for that shit later. Right now, all he cared about was Vanessa and the life she carried.

"One of your demons has what is mine," Death informed Lucifer through gritted teeth.

"What?" Lucifer and Cosmo asked in unison.

"Ezekiel ventured forth to obtain the key to my realm. He also took the one thing I value more than my own existence. My Vanessa."

With the demon's name spoken, Ezekiel fell in a bloody and broken mess at Lucifer's feet, swiftly followed by Deidre, who skidded to a halt when she realized where she was.

Lucifer looked from Ezekiel to Deidre

and raised an eyebrow, "Care to explain your action, flesh eater?"

Deidre rose from all fours to bow her head, "I am sorry for the interruption my Lord. I'll just take my gift and go. I will return later and clean up the mess when you're not so busy." She glanced sideways at Death, then in Cosmo's direction before taking a step towards Ezekiel's whimpering form.

Ezekiel's hands closed around Lucifer's ankle, "Mmm…mmmm…mmm" his lips pressed to the top of Lucifer's foot before he lost consciousness.

Lucifer narrowed his eyes, "Who gifted you, Ezekiel?"

Deidre cowered, "I... Um," she clenched her fist at her sides knowing her answer would lead her into the shit with Lucifer if she said nothing, or even worse, from Leviathan if she confessed to what she knew.

The demographics of the room changed yet again as Leviathan inserted himself into the equation.

CHAPTER 21

Leviathan had spent centuries, too many to remember, planning for this one moment in time when all things would align. The details couldn't have played out any better than they currently were. It was a fucking happy day in Hell, at least for him.

"Lucifer," he sneered at the Dark Lord, "Soul Eater and Cosmo, how convenient. All the heavy hitters are here. Let's get this party started shall we?" He grinned, showing his jagged teeth. "Lucifer you will hand over your key to the underworld and leave immediately. You'll search out your fallen brethren and find a mirror to stand in front of," he snickered. "Cosmo you will stay the butt fuck out of my realm once I am named king. The sight of you offends me, and the smell of you disgusts my senses and puts me off my food. Now for the ceremony of ceremonies," he raised his hand. When it reached waist height, a black dagger with a ruby handle appeared. "You, Soul Eater, you will bring all souls to me in exchange for the life of your wife and your unborn spawn growing in her belly."

Cosmo gasped, "Death, sweetheart?" Cosmo knew that her son would give up his own existence to save that of the woman he loved.

* * *

Vanessa was startled when a soft hand covered her head. When she opened her eyes, the man before her glowed, lighting up the darkest corners of the cavern. He offered her his hand. "Take it, my child. Your Goddess has asked that I come to take you home." He smiled to himself; he really did admire the human's barter system. "Let's get you out of here shall we?"

One moment, Vanessa was in a pit of despair and the next she was standing in a room she recognized to be in Death's realm. "I'm sorry, I must have missed your name, but thank you."

God simply offered a letter, an initial, "G." and with a nod, he imploded into a ball of light and vanished.

* * *

God appeared in Lucifer's throne room with a blinding flash of light. His hand wrapped around Leviathan's palm holding the ceremonial dagger. "Silence!" his voice echoed off the rock walls. "The fate of the world rests in your hands Reaper of Souls, whom do you choose? The love of one woman, or the souls of many?"

Death's stomach knotted at having to make that sort of choice. His chest ached, and his body swayed with the enormity of what he was about to give up. 'I love you, Vanessa,' he whispered softly in his mind, wishing that no matter where she was, she would know he would always love her. "It is my sworn duty to protect and serve. I cannot justify sentencing the entire human race to an existence that is not their true fate. I must sacrifice my own desires and needs for the sake of the many." He fell to his knees in a ruined state.

God's eyes turned an opaque white, and he began to speak in tongues, plunging the dagger into Leviathan's chest. In a swirl of black smoke, his body disintegrated, and the hilt of the blade turned from ruby to onyx. With a spin on the balls of his feet and the agility of a well-weathered warrior, he turned and hurled the dagger end over end at the hellhound trying to inconspicuously retreat from everyone's view. She too became a puff of smoke and was absorbed by the dagger. The hilt again started to change in color, but before it had time to complete the transition, it was flung through the air with the swipe of God's fist. Ezekiel had regained consciousness and was attempting to crawl across the slate floor, his screech was cut short as the dagger dropped to the floor, spun, and then vanished.

God's eyes returned to their crystalline blue, and he looked at the young man emotionally broken on his knees. "Death, rise and be rewarded for your sacrifice." When he didn't move, God moved into a position where he could be seen and heard. He rested his hand on Death's head. "This day I give a reprieve from your duties. Nobody will die today, and nobody will be born. Return to the sanctuary of your realm." Death left to sink into his sorrows as he was dismissed.

God turned to where Lucifer and Cosmo stood. The fact that Lucifer's hand was possessively wrapped around Cosmo's waist did not go unnoticed. Purposefully striding to stand in front of them, he lifted both his hands. Cosmo looked at Lucifer for his reaction, and with a brief nod of his head, he placed his hand inside God's hand closest to him. Cosmo followed his lead, sliding hers inside the other. God lifted Cosmo's hand to his lips and brandished the back of her knuckles with a kiss. He smirked with satisfaction as he then did the same with Lucifer's, "The power of three are reunited."

* * *

Vanessa had made her way to the bathroom and removed all her clothes. She wrinkled her nose at the putrid ash that covered them. Stepping under the hot water of the shower, she scrubbed herself clean and washed her hair. Unable to focus on anything or anyone, she couldn't even fathom where the hell Reaper could be. Exhaustion quickly overtook her, and she dried herself off quickly and climbed into the king size bed. No sooner had Vanessa's head hit the pillow than she allowed sleep to take her.

Death materialized in his study, falling into his chair behind his desk. He had never felt so lost or in so much pain before. Opening the desk drawer, he pulled out a bottle of Silver Patron and a shot glass. Not willing to set eyes on the table in the kitchen where he'd made Vanessa cum for him, he filled the shitty little glass, silently wishing the top of the bottle was a little more slug friendly. A full bottle of tequila later and still aching for his wife, he pitched the elegantly shaped, thick glass bottle at the fireplace. He had no desire to ever see his bed again either. He had no doubt that it would still smell of her natural scent.

Closing his eyes, he tried to ignore the

tingle that indicated he was close to losing the argument of big guys don't cry when a soft hand cupped his jawline. "Reaper?"

Death squeezed his eyes tightly closed, not willing to risk the possibility that his mind was playing tricks on him. "Baby?" Vanessa pleaded. Death's entire body began to tremble and the tears he'd been fighting so hard to hold back leaked from the corners of his closed eyes.

"Shhh, I'm here," she said planting kisses on his face as she straddled his lap. His sobs wracking his body, he slowly lifted his arms, wrapping them around her waist and pulling her in close. Death's memory of her felt so real it was killing him.

He buried his head between Vanessa's breasts and began to mumble over and over, "I'm sorry." She felt so real, her skin was soft and warm. He moaned when she ran her tongue along the shell of his ear. If this were the only way he could keep her memory alive, then he would give into it. His body hardened as his Vanessa teased his earlobe with her teeth.

Vanessa had no idea about the reason

behind Death's traumatized state, but the only thing she knew how to do was to show him that she was here for him and that she loved him.

"I love you Reaper."

CHAPTER 22

Asmodeus stood behind a beautiful blonde. He could see her reflection in the mirrored glass behind the bar, and she was gorgeous. He couldn't put his finger on it, but there was something different about this female. Stepping up closer, the fallen charged with lust brushed against her thigh as he leaned over her shoulder to pay for her drink. She gave him a smile that he felt all the way down to his soul and when she leaned in, her lips brushed his ear. She licked her lips before speaking over the loud music, "I hope you don't think that's going to get you into my panties!" Raising the glass, Asmodeus watched her lick the salt from the back of her hand, knock the shot back and then shove the piece of lemon into the open neck of her Corona. Tapping the necks of both their beers, she saluted him and walked away. Asmodeus was gobsmacked and highly offended. He'd just met the first and only woman that had shot him down. He rubbed his chest. 'Ouch!' he thought to himself, wanting her even more than he did before she'd put on her defiant little show.

* * *

Growing concerned for Death's mental stability, Vanessa ran her hands up into his hair and grabbed two fists full, pulling him back far enough so that she could taste his lips. "Open your fucking eyes Reaper. Look at me. If you love me, you will look at me when you bury your cock inside your wife." She bit his jawline to get his full attention, "As the mother of your child, I command you to look at me."

Death's eyes flashed open, and he gaped at the naked beauty of his redheaded angel in his lap. "Oh God, you're real," he cried tightening his hold on her as he lifted her to the desk in front of him as he stood.

"Oh no you don't, not this time. I want a bed where it's nice and soft," she shook her head.

In the blink of an eye, her back was lowered to the mattress, and Death's naked torso was brushing her erect nipples. He lowered his forehead to rest against hers. "I thought I'd lost you," he said, as he tested her readiness to take him.

Vanessa's breathing increased, and a tear escaped her misty eyes, "I thought I'd lost you too."

Death dipped the head of his shaft in between her folds, then ran it up and over her clit several times. Only when Vanessa began to whimper in his arms did he bury himself deep inside her vessel. His strokes were long and slow as he made passionate love to the woman he thought he would never see again. He had forever to love her, and he had no intentions of rushing things now that she was safely where she belonged... in his heart and in his mind... soul to soul... in his bed.

ABOUT THE AUTHOR

Melissa Bell is a USA Today Best Selling Author who lives in Brisbane, Australia. At a point in her life where she felt she needed something just for herself, she discovered the pleasures of writing. Her most frequently used comment to herself is there's not enough time in a day. She enjoys good food and good company, when she's not trying to concentrate on her writing. She also loves to laugh and most of the time, she cracks herself up. She is hoping that this is the start of something amazing and one day aspires to be listed amongst those blessed with the title of being on the New York Times Best Sellers list.

When she isn't writing she loves to read, many of which she has read over and over again while listening to her favorite Australian bands - Birds of Tokyo and Karnivool.

Please keep an eye out for other books by Melissa Bell.

Stay safe and thank you for reading my book.

ALSO BY MELISSA BELL

Five Brothers Series

Book#1 Houston
Book#2 Felan
Book#3 Tate
Book #4 Channon
Book #4 5 Lupe
(First story in 'Compilation'- A Collection
of Short Stories)
Book #5 London
Books still to come in this series include –
Blaez and Brody amongst others.
(So stay tuned)

Dutiful Gods Series

Book #1 Destiny's Fate
Book #2 Taming Destruction
Book #3 Morpheus's Dream
Book #4 Defying Death
Book #5 Cosmo (TBA)